UnderSurface

a novel

Mitch Cullin

art by
Peter I. Chang

THE PERMANENT PRESS
Sag Harbor, NY 11963

Library of Congress Cataloging-in-Publication Data

Cullen, Mitch
    UnderSurface /by Mitch Cullen
      p. cm.
    ISBN 1-57962-077-9 (alk paper)
    1. Undercover operations-Fiction. 2. Police murders--Fiction.
    3. Married men--Fiction. 4. Gay men--Fiction. I. Title

    PS3553.U319 U53 2002
    813'.54--dc21   2001036621
                                       CIP

Printed in the United States of America

THE PERMANENT PRESS
4170 Noyac Road
Sag Harbor, NY 11963

for Kiyoshi Kurosawa

BOOKS BY MITCH CULLIN

Whompyjawed
Branches
Tideland
The Cosmology Of Bing
From The Place In The Valley Deep In The Forest

With gratitude to the following for support, advice, friendship, and inspiration: Ai, Bill Bishop, Brian Bouldrey, Ellen Bradbury-Reid, Richard Bradford, Kevin Burleson, Joey Burns, Neko Case, The Christians (Charise, Craig, Cameron, Caitlin), John Convertino, Barbara Cooper, Elise D'Haene, Robert Drake, Allyson Edelhertz, Demetrios Efstratiou, Max Evans, Horton Foote, Mary Gaitskill, Howe Gelb, Terry Gilliam, Jemma Gomez, Tony Grisoni, Amon Haruta, Bill Hicks, Tony Hillerman, Ha Jin, Burt Kennedy, Jesiah King, Steve King, Tom Lavoie, Jim Lewis, Nez, John Nichols, Bill Oberdick, The Parras (Chay, Mark, Callen), A. Chad Piper, Robert Phillips, Andy Quan, Colleen Rae, Charlotte & Michael Richardson, Charlotte Roybal, Renee Severin, Tiphanie Shaw, Martin & Judith Shepard, Clay Smith, Marah Stets, Edward Swift, Cole Thompson, Carol Todd, Jeff Tweedy, Kurt Wagner, Mike Walsh, Jane Roberts Wood, Nancy Yamano, Akira Yoshimura, Scott Zesch—and, of course, Peter I. Chang and Brad Thompson and my father Charles Cullin.

Whatsoever ye have spoken in darkness shall be heard in the light; and that which ye have spoken in the ear in closets shall be proclaimed upon the housetops.

—Luke 12:13

I. Under

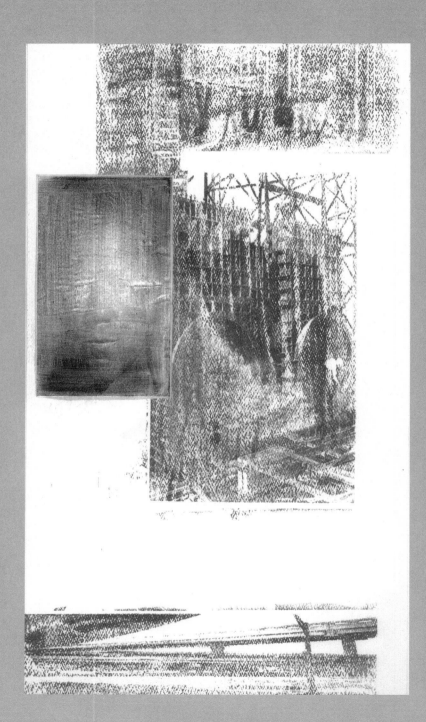

THIS MAN sits upright and, for a brief time, is bemused by the fact that there are people hiding beneath the streets, moving underneath the earth. He knows these subterraneans are glimpsed on occasion, spotted as they emerge into daylight—eyes squinting, so pale even during summertime, visibly uncomfortable below the hard blue sky—as if their vagabond bodies had at last found a homeland within the curves of drainage tunnels, the dank and pitch of concrete intestines: that trickling water, that incessant drip drip drip. Some have spent years migrating from tunnel to tunnel, staking out new territory, venturing above ground only when necessary, growing old while navigating those manmade caverns; others visit the tunnels briefly, never going too far in, remaining until better weather arrives or until whatever trouble hounding them passes—*tourists*, they are sometimes called by more committed underd-wellers.

Tourist—how the word is spoken with such contempt, uttered by men and women who, concealed amongst shadowy environs, gaze reluctantly toward light. Tourist: the one silhouetted in the tunnel's bright mouth, peering at the darkness before cautiously stepping inside with his or her backpack. Like most tourists, these visitors soon treat the tunnels as their own, creating messes, often talking louder than anyone else; they are usually restless souls, discontent, belonging elsewhere but impelled underground.

For example, take this same man—unwashed and foul smelling, bearded, possessing almost nothing from his recent past; a slender, balding man whose body won't settle into the winter night, whose mind can't rest. Nearby, a camp fire ravages kindling, sounding like fall leaves crushed by boots, and Tobias, his elderly companion, snores from a flimsy Lion King sleeping bag. Still, the man is awake, pondering once again the circumstances which have brought him here.

He thinks: I've slept on clean sheets, on a wide mattress, in my own house.

Now unable to slumber, he finally leaves his orange sleeping bag and skirts the fire, abandoning the warmth and escaping Tobias' voluminous breathing. He wanders out along the quiet arroyo, inhaling dry desert air while stargazing, exhaling steam as the heavens flicker.

Then for a moment—when catching sight of a shooting star, a greenish meteor streaking overhead before disappearing altogether—he feels elated, forgetting his waywardness, or that he is being hunted; he forgets where he's been and what he's done—disregards the opening in the earth behind him, that circular shaft winding miles beneath the surface.

But the man isn't alone in that solitary place. Besides himself and Tobias, at least three others occupy the tunnel—a woman of indeterminate age, adorned by scarves and a red bandanna; a Mexican wino, pockets crammed with half-empty pint bottles, whispering continually as he leaves in the afternoon to panhandle for change; a sullen drifter named Tom, his forearms an elaborate display of light-blue tattoos (swastikas, blazing skulls, Virgin Marys); all inhabiting deeper recesses. Like him, they wish to be unbothered, to roam freely, no questions asked.

Sometimes the woman yells inexplicably (her incomprehensible protests traveling and echoing along the shaft walls), or Tom calmly whistles "Lovesick Blues" as if it is his personal invocation during the peaceful moments following sunrise. Though usually he hears very little down here, except the tenor of Tobias' elaborate snoring, the distant rumble of rush hour vehicles zooming about on the highway up above, the campfire pops and crackles, the crickets and infrequent coyote yip yaps.

Camping at the tunnel's entrance, beyond which stretches sand and gravel, he has grown accustomed to the others stepping over his sleeping bag at all hours, journeying outside to rummage through dumpsters behind fast food chains, hoping for sacks of unsold hamburgers or Hefty bags containing stale bagels and moldy bread. As for him, he finds meals at Safeway, in the evening when the store is crowded. Lately, he's become quite deft at slipping cans of Campbell's into his overcoat pockets, a master at shoving sacks of fresh tortillas underneath his shirt, snug against his waistline. Twice a week he strolls those busy aisles—casually maneuvering between shopping carts, grim housewives and complaining children—his fingers reaching here and there, darting like a viper's tongue from long sleeves. He always returns to the tunnel well supplied.

"The foodman cometh," Tobias said yesterday, rising from where he sat cross-legged. "Whatcha got for us, buddy? Whatcha carrying there?"

Soups, tortillas, candy bars, cheese slices—materializing like magic, appearing from pockets, shaken from pants legs.

"And just for you, my friend—"

A shiny Granny Smith apple, held in a palm, extended toward Tobias' grinning face.

"Now ain't that somethin'—ain't that the damnedest thing—you're a keeper, buddy, you really are—"

With missing front teeth, a jaw displaying blackened molars, Tobias would need to cut the apple into manageable slices, eventually sucking each one until the meat was soft enough to chew—a time-consuming process. Nevertheless, the old guy proudly rubbed the apple against his shirt, sniffed it, then licked at the waxy skin and grinned.

"The details of a thing, buddy—the stuff we ignore is what matters, ain't that right?"

The man nodded, shrugging his shoulders.

Tobias' gaze stayed on him, as if a more appropriate response was expected.

"Ain't that right, huh?"

"Sure, probably."

"Ain't it though?"

"Sure."

Tobias, his rusty can opener hanging off a silver chain around his neck, is rarely unpleasant. He never complains much, seems glad for whatever companionship and food gets offered, is clearly pleased with their arrangement; he lets the man use his extra sleeping bag, allows him to sip from his gallon water jug, shares the warmth of his fires— in exchange, the man brings him nourishment, none of it dug from trash bins.

"Good eats," Tobias says again and again, drops of tomato soup glistening throughout his curly gray beard. "Good good eats in the age of Gotam, and the starvation of American cattle, that's for sure, you know what I'm sayin'—"

Of course, Tobias is mentally unstable, although kind and harmless; the man immediately realized this about him the afternoon they met in Papago Park. The old guy didn't have to speak a single word, or explain his idea of breeding cows with massive zippers sewn along their sides ("Buddy, they can't die—go unzip them, get all the meat you want, zip her back up—not a single soul starves. The government is workin' on it—on makin' fresh meat grow back in livin' Herefords—genetic engineerin'—they're doin' it in Brazil right now, ha!"). No, a quick glance at the mumbling vagrant could have told him everything—two baseball caps on his head, one on top of the other, barefoot, frayed jean cuffs rolled to scabby knees.

When Tobias first approached the man, he was searching for a dog named Tina. "She's my bitch, you know.

You can call a dog a bitch, as long as it's a bitch, right? It's okay doing that. I mean, don't go callin' anyone else that, especially a bitch that ain't a dog. Christ, that'll rain a heap of trouble on your head if you go and do that—I ain't kiddin'." The man asked what the dog looked like, what breed—and Tobias' face became puzzled when he replied: "Can't really say—she ran off in Phoenix a while back, maybe Tempe. Sort of a little happy dog, pretty eyes, real energetic. Boy, she ran fast, that little dog—that bitch."

You're insane, the man thought. You're nuts.

Except now the nut case is his only comrade, and he's thankful for his odd company: "Buddy, ain't a soul breathing who don't require some form of kinship—don't have to be a big deal, maybe an animal, a tree would work—'cept I think another human voice helps, don't you?" Furthermore, if Tobias hadn't shown him the tunnel ("Plenty warm down there, fairly cozy, you'll see"), hadn't loaned him his other sleeping bag ("Mi bag es your bag, got it?"), he'd still be hiding in the park somewhere, shuddering all night beneath his overcoat, praying for sleep on a bench, using his hands as a pillow.

Yet Tobias' generosity betrays a greater loneliness; the man sensed this soon after moving into the tunnel. Whenever he leaves to steal their groceries, Tobias invariably asks him, "Say, you'll be comin' back, won't you?"

Upon his return, Tobias often leaps toward him with arms outstretched: "Got worried, buddy, I did—you been gone a spell."

In quieter moments, as the two sit around the fire sipping coffee, the man has glanced at Tobias' forlorn expression; he has seen the inwardness, the fear and solitude barely hidden by those watery gray eyes.

What pain brought you here? the man has wondered. What damaged you so?

No apparent answers were forthcoming, nothing really learned regarding the old vagrant's history—just this:

"Since a kid I've valued my human connections. Mother was like that too. She'd bring folks inside our house, them lacking homes, headed from someplace to someplace else—gave 'em a dinner, a towel for their face. She'd tell me, 'Son, we ain't no different, all of us is connected, you give kindness to a lost soul and you're givin' it to yourself—could easily be you blowin' along the road needin' comfort sometime.'

"See, the way I figure it—a man wants someone close, someone to let him know he's alive, right? A friend, a pal. Buddy, I've had me lots, tons of friends. They'll stay a day or two, sometimes a week. I get 'em down here, get food in 'em, and we don't got to talk a whole bunch. Shit, we don't got to talk at all—so long as I can see his face, he can see mine. Makes a difference, you know. It sure does. A life gets pretty bleak without your friends, ain't that true? Ain't it?"

Then last week Tobias introduced a new friend to the tunnel: a teenager named Mike—left eyebrow pierced, black hair bleached white, sixteen, almost as tall as a college basketball player, although far too skinny for good health. His parents had kicked him out because, the boy claimed, they were sick of his shit (his shit being truancy, petty theft, and a minor drug problem involving weed and drinks pilfered from his dad's wet bar). Tobias found him shivering on a park bench, and, after promising food and a warmer refuge, persuaded Mike to come with him.

"Was worried at first that Tobias was a faggot," Mike later told the man while they foraged for kindling. "Thought he'd try sucking my dick or something else creepy—but he's all right, I guess."

"He's fine—a little weird sometimes. He means well though."

They had paused beside a lightning-charred saguaro, where the boy squatted and blew breath between his cupped hands. Beyond them, the desert—scattered with ocotillos and creosote bushes and stately saguaros—sloped upward to the Tucson mountains. Several miles behind them, a haze of chimney smoke hung over the city, which, like the boy's breath, was faint and gauze-like.

"Fuck, dude, it's cold."

The man too was blowing into his own hands, rubbing them together. And even though the sun was hot on their necks, neither produced a drop of sweat or felt his skin burning.

"How does Tobias do it?" said Mike, shaking his head. "How does he survive and not freeze to death? I'd die if I lived like this very long."

"Well, I don't think he's stupid," the man said, turning away. "I mean, we're the ones doing the dirty work and he's still sleeping. I think he's got it all worked out somehow— he'd have to." He ambled forward, scanning the earth for anything worth collecting—dry grass, bark, newspaper blown from the city to the desert.

"That's true," Mike said, standing upright and following. "Like you say, he probably isn't stupid. You know, I bet he's hardly crazy either. I bet it's mostly an act and he's like all smart and shit. Like maybe he's one of those physicist guys who flipped and decided it's better getting back to basics. Seriously, he looks smart—in a messed up, goofy kind of way—"

But the man wasn't listening anymore. Instead, while reaching for a rotting piece of ironwood, he began pondering Mike's disposition. As a high school English teacher, he had dealt regularly with troubled, moody boys like him—kids who were, for the most part, decent yet contrary, gentle in their own ways.

In Mike's case, he saw through the adolescent swagger, the crass language, the insecure bluster—underneath it all existed a benevolent and sensitive nature that, on occasion, became obvious: a day earlier, when ants invaded their stash of Heath bars, the boy meticulously fashioned a thin trail of honey, leading the hungry swarm into the arroyo;

more than once, the man awoke to what he first discerned as the boy giggling, only to realize Mike was crying quietly near the diminishing camp fire. And if the boy had been his child, his teenager, he would never have thrown him so carelessly into the world. No, he would have discussed things with him, weighing their problems, searching for productive and less harsh solutions. That's what he always did with his own boy, he discussed things.

"David, there's not a problem we can't manage," he'd often told his eight-year-old son when some minor drama erupted (a broken window, baseball cards stolen from the grocery store, a goldfish put inside the microwave). "There's nothing you can't tell me or ask me, okay?"

"Okay," David would say, nodding assuredly, comforted in his father's hugging arms.

The man suspected that Mike's dad was quite different, probably reluctant to wrap his arms around his son's narrow body, or to sit him down at a garage worktable, showing him how to build an airplane from scrap lumber. He was positive Mike rarely heard those essential words spoken by his father's lips, that heartfelt whispering: "I love you, you mean everything to me."

Too bad, he thought. A shame.

"So what's your story?" Mike asked the man, stepping alongside him, watching as he stomped the branches of a fallen mesquite tree.

"Don't have one, sorry."

The man gave the boy an askance glance and smiled.

"Come on, that's not true. Everyone does."

"Everyone," the man said, short of breath, "except me." His left boot paused amongst the splintered gray branches. He inhaled tiredly, patting Mike on the shoulder. "Mind helping me do this?"

"Yeah, I don't mind."

Then they both started stomping, splintering limbs, pounding the tree apart—delighting in the havoc, the crack and snap and crushing of brittle wood.

Like father and son, the man imagined. Like two of a kind. And, he believed, it didn't matter what had been reported about him (pervert, killer, monster of the worst kind), because no one could ever regard him as a bad father—not his wife, his son or his daughter, or even the police.

Additionally, he was a selfless educator, an involved teacher who, every Monday and Wednesday, had read about each of his students; their bi-weekly journal entries usually revealing much more than was expected (fear of failing grades, sexual interests, sudden desperation, fathomless angst). They could write with complete impunity, it was promised, and he acted as an eager sounding board for their ruminations. In this manner his students valued him, depended on him. He was a lot more than Mr. Connor; he was an ally to their fantasies and desires. He had gradually earned their trust—and, in time, he would surely gain Mike's trust. By next week, the man reasoned, you and I will be simpatico—you'll share your worries and regrets, perhaps I'll confide mine.

Except it wasn't meant to happen: the boy stayed for four nights and three days—then he vanished at dawn, stealing a few Twinkies and a loaf of bread and the man's wallet.

"Here yesterday," said Tobias, "bye today."

And while the loss of his wallet was discouraging, the man was also somewhat relieved to be freed from such a bulging reminder of his past—relieved too that, weeks earlier, he had burnt his credit cards, bank receipts, and driver's license, doing so to protect his identity in case his wallet fell into the wrong hands. But, for whatever reasons, Mike left the only two items the man continued to treasure, both extracted from the wallet and placed beside his sleeping bag—a Sears family portrait taken last summer (the man standing with his wife, his hands placed on his children's necks), and his American Model Society

17

membership card (advantages: discounts at Hobby House, monthly news digests, a VIP subscription to *American Model*).

So now on this night—as the man stands by himself in the arroyo, gazing upward at pricks of starlight marking the wide dark canopy of sky—he's hoping Mike gets good use from the wallet, though he can't understand why the boy bothered stealing it (there was no cash, no credit cards, nothing of value other than what was left behind). In a way, he's sorry about destroying the credit cards because they might have helped the boy out. Nonetheless, the man knows it's all for the best—if Mike had used any of the cards, had bought just a Coke or chewing gum, then a troublesome chain of events would surely unfold (the police would find the boy, the boy would admit where the wallet came from).

Inexperienced criminals, the man already figured, probably utilize their own plastic for a cheap hotel room and a proper meal, swiping the card once and dumbly revealing their whereabouts—but he isn't that idiotic; he isn't that witless.

Better to burn the cards, he concludes. Much better than letting Mike use them. Still, the man wishes he and the boy had talked at some length; he wishes he'd urged him to return home, or at least to find a safe environment where he could live.

"Stay in the light," he should have advised him. "Avoid suspect men, avoid shadowy places."

That's what he'd say if the boy were here tonight.

That, he thinks, is what someone should've said to me.

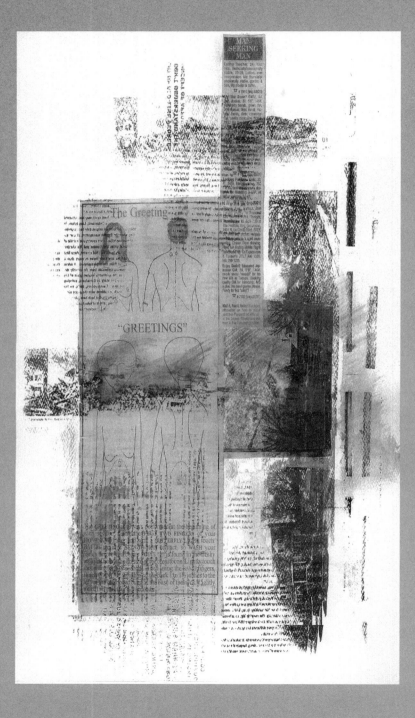

WHEN WANDERING the arroyo late at night, the man inevitably becomes aware of creatures rustling bushes and darting across his path—field mice or roving jackrabbits or ground squirrels; it's difficult telling for certain in the dark. Other times he has stopped cold in his tracks, thinking for a moment that his name has been spoken as a faint whisper—the words carried by the breeze or called from behind mesquite trees several yards away. He has heard footsteps crunching behind him in the sand, but, turning swiftly around, finds himself alone. Or he'll hear a jet rumbling through the sky, sometimes catch indistinct voices shouting from the nearby park, perhaps even pause a moment to shut his eyes while listening to traffic whooshing up on the highway (vehicles coming and going sporadically, sounding like the abating of a fast wind).

Just now a car throbs with heavy bass, and he envisions southside teenagers taking a midnight drive, escaping the city, headlights aimed westward as they cruise toward the desert, transporting rap music and beer cans into a scraggy landscape lorded over by towering saguaros. Once beyond Papago Park, the road they drive will soon narrow, quickly becoming curvy and upwardly sloping, eventually dead-ending at an overlook parking lot—from that vantage point everything below appears like above, thousands of lights floating and twinkling in an expanse of blackness.

The man knows the overlook well, having flown a remote-control plane there during springtime, on weekend afternoons when the valley, town, and outskirt places—such

21

as Papago Park and this arroyo—appeared both faraway and proximate. He also had sex there one summer's night, moaning loudly at the second of release, eyes wide open and fixed on the city's incandescence—a scattershot of blues, yellows, and whites which somehow seemed intangible to him. He remembers feeling very little connection or affinity with those familiar streets and buildings of the city. How odd to realize now, while returning to the tunnel, that his sense of detachment isn't any more profound tonight than back then; it's as if he has always existed obscurely down here, as if a secret part of himself has always been moving and pissing and slumbering in the tunnel since the day he was born.

"Bein' birthed is a tricky thing," he recalls Tobias suddenly saying, as if furthering some profound and serious conversation. "Got no notion of where you came from, no say where you find yourselves." He poked at the fire with a stick, agitating cinders. "Hell, don't pay me any mind," he continued. "I think too much. 'Cept I'm thinkin' you're birthed and you grow older and you shuffle around and you got no notion of why exactly you're shuffling around at all, know what I mean?"

"I get the general idea," the man replied, doing his best to follow. "You're wondering what the reason is? What's the meaning?"

"Well, yes and no."

Tobias began talking about reincarnation, inanimate objects possessing souls, parallel universes, in a somber, methodical, sincere way. He seemed to have spent a great deal of time meditating on the subjects; at least he sounded like he had. Finally, out of curiosity, the man asked if he believed in life after death.

"Sure enough," Tobias responded, "but who's to say there ain't life before birth? Who's to say theys ain't gone and lived a hundred different lifetimes in a blink and never known one from the other?"

"Maybe so," the man said.

Humans were foot soldiers, Tobias continued. Men and women were always expendable, he explained. "God's army is a limitless thing, so it don't matter who comes and who goes, right? One ain't no different than another—especially us men—we come and go the easiest—that's on account that we're born out as soldiers, I think. That's why we lose our way in this world sometimes—without that fighting and them wars we don't belong, see? A comfortable society eats at us, makes us crazy—that's on account we can't birth babies—that's on account we was made to serve and fight things—that's how we get to that God, serving and fighting and all that—and without that we're like shells, ain't that so? Either way you cut it we're trumped."

It is a cold night, breezy, the air scented from the mesquite branches feeding the fire. The man stretches out on his sleeping bag, combing his beard with soiled fingertips. By firelight he can see Tobias resting on his back, arms along his sides, belly rising and falling beneath his torn Harley-Davidson T-shirt, mouth agape and releasing a harsh snoring—a guttural commotion, a pleading of sorts, loud enough to spook bobcats or pumas; the resonance of it never fails to summon the man's wife Julie. And like Tobias' racket, her nightly gasps and grumbles fueled his growing insomnia.

But during their first few years of marriage the snoring wasn't an issue; they slept peacefully, his body spooning her body, their legs intertwined.

"I love you," he would whisper in the morning, holding her.

"Love you too," she would reply, reaching to touch his face.

Sometimes he would slide a hand between her legs, letting his fingers prowl. "Oh god, I love you—"

Then having slept contentedly, they would kiss one another fervently.

She would bite his earlobe, she would suck his tongue. "Fuck me," she would say. "Please, fuck me," and he would.

Like waking from a blissful dream, he imagines, and finding yourself in the middle of a wonderful fantasy. Only later, after the birth of their second child, did her grating snoring invade and alter his dreaming, manifesting in various forms—a jar of bees, a dog growling behind a chain-link fence, his late grandfather trying so desperately to swallow with his cancer-ridden throat—until, at last, he'd awake miserably beside her: "Julie—! Julie, you're snoring!"

"What—?"

"You're snoring again."

"Are you sure?"

"Yes, I'm sure."

One morning over breakfast Julie explained it like this: "Since Monica was born, you know I've gained a lot of weight. That's the whole problem, I'm sure. Fat collects at the neck and throat, that's the cause. So if you can survive three months, you'll see, I'll lose it—I promise you."

Except within two months she was bigger—within six months she had reached obesity. Then it seemed that as her appetite grew, so did her clamorous nocturnal breathing. Most nights he retreated to the guest room; weekend nights he watched television downstairs; sometimes he worked on his model airplanes in the garage.

"I'm sorry," his wife repeatedly said. "You're so patient with me, and I appreciate it. I love you, I really do."

"I love you too. Don't worry."

"Thank you," she said. "It's hard, I know—but I'll fix it. I hate thinking something as stupid as snoring could hurt us."

"It won't," he reassured her. "I mean, it's a problem, just not a major problem."

No, not a major problem, because soon the need for sleep abandoned him even when he couldn't hear his wife's gasps—even in the quiet of the guest bedroom, or when reclining on the living room couch—even wearing earplugs that, aside from his own heart's steady beating, muted every noise, every cough, snort, creak.

He thinks: Julie, I can't blame you for anything—any more than I can blame you for the terrible predicament I've found myself in.

He believes she isn't responsible for what he did while she slept (her lips parted and purring with such awful volume, her nostrils flared), the hours he spent driving about the city, radio cranked, unsure of where weariness would claim him—paused at a red light on an otherwise empty street, filling his gas tank before sunrise, or while Julie started breakfast and he sat waiting for his eggs.

"Honey, is everything okay? You're looking haggard."

"I'm fine."

"You'd tell me if anything was wrong."

"Absolutely. Trust me, I'm fine, honestly."

Just restlessness, he thought then.

He knows better than that now. It wasn't restlessness pulling him into the night. Restlessness didn't open that murky fissure in his mind, making his home and family and job feel numbing, hardly enlivening: how impossible to give it a name, let alone explain it to those who loved him; how difficult to find definition or logic as it seized him by degrees, drawing him in until what it presented became so alluring and so essential. Something else, he understands, something desultory—but not restlessness. And not snoring; with or without Julie's rhythmic grumbling, he'd still be exactly where he is tonight—in this tunnel, at the arroyo, near the park. The end result would surely be the same, he knows.

Nevertheless, he wishes she had caught him once stepping out the front door at midnight, or had at least confronted him upon an early morning return—as he tidied himself up, as he readied for an exhausting day of teaching

Shakespeare. She could have asked where he had been, demanding answers, glaring at him with suspicion. Then perhaps he might have curbed his roving—those increasingly dark drives which propelled him farther and farther away from home. But she remained without suspicion, always smiling when he came to breakfast.

"How'd you sleep?"

He'd nod, always saying, "Good."

"Do you want orange juice, apple juice?"

He envied her belief in the sanctity of their marriage, her absolute trust of him. No cruel secrets, nothing hidden. To her, he appeared as she willed him to be: a decent father, uncomplicated, incapable of hurting himself or her or their children, never one to behave wantonly; he wouldn't trip selfishly over his own feet.

Yet he would trip, and he would hurt—unintentionally, of course. He doesn't believe it was a deliberate downward spiral, or that he ever put himself at serious peril. Still, if there was indeed a fall, a collapse, then it commenced at Greasewood Palace, a twenty-four-hour adult arcade located a few blocks from his house. Even so, the place wasn't a mystery to him or Julie: twice they had ventured inside with hopes of improving their declining sex life, although the purchase of a thick black dildo and mint-flavored whipped cream, novelty items at best, did very little to enhance their lackluster lovemaking.

So when entering the shop by himself one sleepless night—apparently self-conscious, looking disheveled after driving for hours—he didn't know what else could be had besides rubber toys, porno magazines, and four day rentals on hardcore videotapes. He hadn't previously noted the whitewashed door which led patrons to the arcade booths (he and Julie never went beyond the book racks and display cases). And if he wasn't sick of driving, of obsessively adhering to an invariable route (back past the high school where he taught, through downtown, past the school again, into the desert, back past the school), or if he hadn't stopped at Circle K for gas, glancing casually across Park Avenue while filling his Suburban, and spotted the large neon sign glowing—GREASEWOOD PALACE—he would have likely resumed the same route.

As it happened his life shifted that night, not in an obvious manner, not significantly, although it did change, he understands now; all it took was five dollars in gold tokens and a whitewashed door swinging toward darkness, bringing him to a narrow corridor lined on either side by six arcade booths: every booth fitted with a lock, a seat wide enough for two, a box of Kleenex, a trashcan, and a multi-channel television delivering as much sex—breasts and vaginas and penises and balls and assholes and spread legs—as any thirty-four-year-old English teacher could ever wish to gaze upon.

That night he stayed for less than ten minutes. He didn't recline on the seat or kneel, didn't scan the fifty-eight channels, didn't use up his tokens; he simply locked himself inside a booth, deposited three tokens into the grimy slot, and continued standing upright.

The man has long since forgotten what exactly was playing when he unzipped his fly, but he does recall the swiftness of his orgasm, the way his sperm erupted thickly and spattered the screen. Suddenly he was awash with embarrassment, thoroughly ashamed while grabbing for tissue. Worse, he began fearing the management might somehow trace who had ejaculated on the television, so he made use of more Kleenex, handfuls, meticulously wiping clean the screen. Rather than throw the tissue into the trashcan, he crammed the wad in a pocket, as if damaging and incriminating evidence could be gathered from its sticky contents—and, head lowered, walked quickly from the booth, the arcade, the store.

On the short drive home, a drug-like stupor overtook him—his eyelids sagged, his legs grew heavy. Soon he was sleeping in the guest bedroom, hardly shifting an inch (chest down, pillow pressed over his head).

Four hours later he stirred—his body completely rested, his mind alert—invigorated by the sunlight shining through the rose-colored curtains; he hadn't slept that soundly in weeks, perhaps months.

"Good morning," he said to himself. "Good—morning."

During his shower he started whistling "All Day And All Of The Night," the song still piping from him as he combed his hair and after he brushed his teeth and while he dressed—remaining with him as he jogged downstairs for breakfast, ceasing only when he entered the kitchen, where he bestowed kisses on Julie and David and Monica (the three sitting at the table, bemused by his jovial entrance).

"Someone's in fine form today," Julie remarked to the children. "Doesn't Daddy look happy today?"

The children nodded, staring abstractly at their father before returning to their Pop Tarts.

As always, the man was the last to sit down at the table and—his mouth chewing a final bite of toast—the first rising to go: another kiss for the children, another kiss for Julie—a smile, and a goodbye.

"See you this evening," he told them, heading for the front door.

By the time he reached the driveway, the street vibrated from commuter traffic. Then, slipping behind the steering wheel, he saw again the images shown in the arcade booth and, with those scenes consuming his thoughts, proceeded toward morning rush hour, whistling while passing suburban homes like his own—those three or four designs and floorplans, the no-wax vinyl floorings, ceramic tile, oak front cabinets, two-car garages, the earth tone exteriors appearing as make-believe adobe. He was oblivious to it all; he was somewhere else, his mind fixed on bodies moving rhythmically against bodies, smooth torsos sweating and long legs wrapping around slender or muscular waists.

When he arrived at the high school, the images lingered and for a while he sat in his vehicle after claiming his parking space, unwilling to move outside until the erection in his pants subsided. Briefly, he tried summoning guilt or at least a degree of shame, but it proved useless; he didn't feel bad, not like he had directly following his Greasewood orgasm—in fact, he felt capricious, nervously vibrant. He considered then what he had known since adolescence: those milliseconds that contained his orgasms, those intense and fleeting moments, were the closest he felt to divinity—yet the minutes afterwards were like some humiliating plunge from grace (how the circle went round and round: that continual grasping toward great heights, that always abrupt fall as the outcome of reaching such rapture).

His fingers fidgeted, drumming the steering wheel. For a moment he attempted to conjure other images, something awful to displace the potent sex scenes in his mind: he envisioned a motorcycle accident once witnessed, the body crumpled against a shattered windshield; he pictured John F. Kennedy's autopsy photographs, the dead president's eyes wide open, the top of his head a mess of torn flesh and hair; ultimately he settled on famine, on Ethiopian children with bloated stomachs, emaciated limbs, brown skin badgered by flies—that did the trick; he could climb out, he could mount the steps and enter the building, moving forward anxiously.

Then teaching his first period English class, while reading *Hamlet* aloud, he sensed a similar discontentment amongst his students—the bouncing knees, the fidgeting fingers, the yawns, the sighs, the continual doodling in notebooks.

"Do you know what Charles Darwin said about Shakespeare?" he asked them. "He said, 'I have tried lately to read Shakespeare, and found it so intolerably dull that it nauseated me,'" which brought several chuckles and utters of agreement from the kids. Finally, he abandoned *Hamlet* altogether, encouraging his students instead to share their happiest memories, a few having interesting tales to relate.

Graham Sweeney discovered ten dollars hidden beneath an old tire one afternoon: "That was the best. I bought like ice creams for my cousins and me—we all hung out downtown, so that was pretty cool."

Angela Groves danced with her grandma along the corridors of a retirement center: "Wasn't like there was no music or anything, but she hummed some song and then showed me like this dance she did when she was my age—we danced slow because she's old—so that's my happiest memory because she was happy, and I cried because I was happy for her."

Pat Kilroy shook Ringo Starr's right hand when encountering the ex-Beatle in a Phoenix mall: "He didn't look too old, seemed nervous, I don't know. I guess after John Lennon and all that I'd be nervous too. But he was nice, except he wouldn't give me an autograph. He said like if he gave me one then everyone would start like wanting one and he'd be stuck there all day. I guess he bought something at The Gap. Thought that was funny—he was carrying a Gap bag. His wife and like these bodyguard guys were like carrying bags too, some shopping spree I guess—at least I think it was his wife, I don't know. He sounds just like he sings, like 'Yellow Submarine'."

At a garage sale, Tim Enchi got a pricey Steve Garvey baseball card for a quarter: "Wasn't in mint condition. I'd say good to very good, not mint. When I showed my dad he was excited for me—he knew I'd wanted that card for a long time."

Camika Estes met her best friend during a Super K-Mart Thanksgiving sale: "We were at the same sale rack, then she reaches for the same pants I was reaching for and we laughed about it—and we kept talking and stuff after that. We like the same stuff, we're like sisters. She's helped me through some hard times—so it's weird to think that K-Mart pretty much changed my life."

Connie Leong found three small bluebirds amongst fireplace soot, unhurt and hungry: "We cleaned them with a towel. They fit in my mom's palm, she could hold two in one hand. Then we drove them over to the vet. Now before we start a fire, we always check. I'd hate it if we ended up burning some other birds up—I'm happy we didn't burn those ones."

Afterwards, the man stood before his students and studied their faces for a moment (such singular expressions, each contained and unique, like fingerprints).

"Thank you," he said, in a solemn, grateful voice. "Thank you for sharing."

Life, it seemed to him, could be curious and rich, full of unexpected gifts in surprising places.

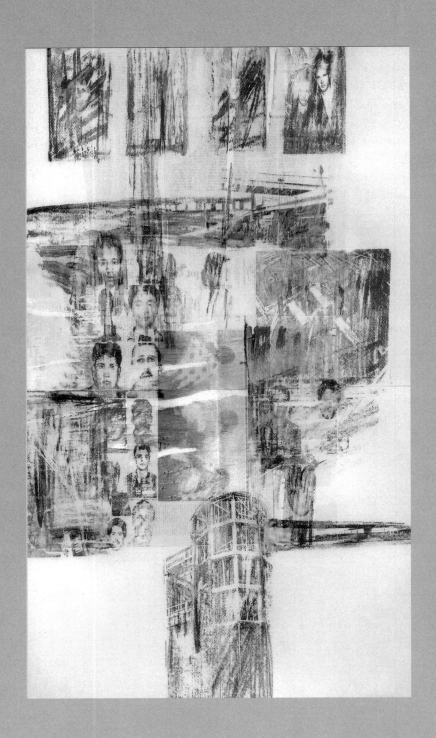

THE MAN has dreamed of his son, the boy reaching to grasp his hand.

David, the fair prince.

David, the firstborn and most beloved.

A shy child, withdrawn, with delicate features—blue eyes, pale skin, voice like a whisper, asking, "Dad, why are there birds in the sky?"

My David.

"Where does rain come from?"

Or his son will find him during sleep, running up alongside him, always reaching, asking his questions.

"Why do flowers die and change color? Where do the colors go?"

The man wished to speak, to beg for forgiveness—but the words were too painful. So better to hold the boy, as he does in dreams. Better to pull him close and saying nothing.

"Dad—"

The boy possessing his father's eyes, though revealing something unsure and rueful in his gaze.

That boy—content working beside his father in the backyard, willing to spend hours inside the garage while watching the man build airplanes from wood.

"Dad—?"

It could awaken any sleeper: the man sitting upright, his hands shaking. Then turning his face from Tobias and the camp fire, he gazed into the darkness of the tunnel.

"I'm sorry," he said to himself, and can say little else.

Suddenly someone spoke his name, uttering it faintly just beyond the tunnel's black mouth.

"Who are you—?" he asked.

Someone moved out in the arroyo—an indistinct form, darting away from him in the night.

"David," he whispered, but knew it wasn't his son. "David," he said again, shutting his eyes and pretending he hadn't heard his name spoken and thinking only of those times his boy had come to him during dreams.

But David isn't the only one who has found him at night. Julie has materialized on occasion, holding Monica— his daughter's arms wrapped around her mother's neck, the two like ghosts, speechless and still, glaring from the front porch. No questions were clearly asked, no sign given— merely the silent condemnation of their sullen faces. Nevertheless, he heard them plainly. In those dreams they were communicating by appearance, telling him everything he'd already inquired of himself.

"I'm sorry—"

He accepted their anger, their confusion; he took their pain and made it his own burden. To them he could speak, perhaps because they would not.

I wanted what I wanted, he thought, except I don't understand why I wanted it. You see I'm human, I'm flawed—it doesn't mean I didn't love you more than anything. I'm just a selfish, stupid man—the world is full of us. This world was fashioned by men wanting what they want without considering the consequences of their desires, you must know that.

"Forgive me, please."

Now he waits for evidence of their forgiveness. The boy he doesn't worry about; David loves him, the dreams reveal this truth. The others, however, he hasn't seen in a while. Julie and Monica. It's been weeks since they entered his slumber, staring at him from the porch. He expects them sometime soon, believes they are forthcoming. How he prays they will look upon him with new expressions— offering grins, waves, maybe blowing kisses.

Take your time, he thinks. I'll be waiting right here—at least until winter passes, until the summer monsoon starts. After the rains, you'll have to find me elsewhere.

Because by midsummer, he is positive, the tunnel will be a dangerous hideaway; for he recalls last summer when the monsoon flooded avenues, bringing record rains, turning dry arroyos into turbulent rivers (killing at least eight); the normally safe and dry drainage tunnels were submerged without warning: "Gotam, God of our syphilization, flushes his toilet," Tobias has warned him, "cleansing the squalor that's got collected here."

All of this—where he rests, the campfire, the tunnel walls, the sand, the arroyo—consumed and put underwater. The nearby desert then becoming a fragrant, sodden oasis (ocotillos blooming, wildflowers sprouting), and the man sees himself out there, wandering away from the tunnel, leaving the city and its people behind. He'll avoid drowning come summer, regardless of how appealing the idea sometimes seems. He'll continue onward for no other reason than that he must.

"That's just what you do," Tobias said. "You keep on keepin' on. That's what we are—on-keepers. You know, every place I've called mine has disappeared. Most of my friends too. Lost two friends and a home at Redrock Wash in a single afternoon. Went off searchin' for Tina, came back after it started pourin'—figured I missed a turn somewhere—won't be the first time, that's the truth—'cause the whole camp, the damn wash and that tunnel I'd called home for eighty-six suns wasn't no more—just gone, buddy, just gone gone gone—made a big ol' bad river, wild and mean, rollin' hard like the Colorado—and know what I was thinkin' then? I was thinkin', hope Fletch weren't passed out when the flood came, hope that other friend—what's-his-name with that bad left leg—hope he's faster than that cruel water—but no no, not a chance, buddy, no no. They get swept away, someone reports they got found south around Nogales, tangled up in some barbered wire that cuts cross them washes there. Two best buddies gone from this sad world, deader than dead, as dead as there is—could be me too, buddy. Could be us too if we're here too long—so do think of that when you're thinkin'."

"I will."

"No kiddin', buddy, ponder on that and tell me there ain't a master plan at work in the universe—'cause for darn sure there is. You busy ponderin' already?"

"I am."

"Can't say I blame you."

Yet for all the ravages of the monsoon season, the man associates the storms of last summer with something besides nature's wrath or as a welcome interlude calming the heat (the clouds having spent the day widening and gathering darkly above the desert while creeping gradually towards the city). To him, the mighty downpours, being so suddenly impious and disastrous, were often an excuse, an explainable reason for coming home later than expected, wet and tired, from whichever jaunt he had embarked on by himself—hiking, grocery shopping, getting the oil changed. The freedom of not teaching in the summer afforded him limitless downtime, and, because of such a luxury, the daily forecasts governed his schedule: clear mornings meant hours of yard work (watering the lemon trees, yanking weeds, planting seeds); partly cloudy middays afforded park trips with his children (playing freeze tag or catch, sometimes swimming); overcast afternoons had him telling Julie that a vital errand had to be taken care of (glue at the hobby shop, overdue library books, videos returned to Blockbuster).

"Be careful," she'd say.

"Always am," he'd reply.

She'd follow him to the front door, making sure he wouldn't forget his umbrella.

"You might need it. Don't want to get caught in the rain again."

"Thanks, I'll try not to."

On the afternoons that rainfall passed the city, he and David would travel to that hilltop overlook, the remote-operated Mark II Lysander they built cradled in his son's small arms as the man drove.

Yet if gray clouds swirled above his house, if distant thunder erupted, rattling windows, he'd waste no time in gathering his car keys, in kissing Julie and saying, "I'll be back, better get it all finished before it gets bad."

Except he never finished his errands ahead of the deluge, that wasn't the plan—and he always returned wearied, worn-out, ready for a long shower and a fast dinner, then an early retreat beneath the covers in the guest bedroom, where he drifted off without effort and awoke without recollecting whatever dreams had visited him.

Still, at the beginning of last summer he considered himself a novice thrill-seeker, escaping his family and his home for short periods, curiously exploring an enticing realm he barely knew (this before discovering the glory holes in the back booths at Greasewood, the blowjobs awaiting him within the public toilet near Mission Park's baseball diamond). In hindsight, he regards that June as an arid, cloudless month which brought him hastily into the adult store after his family had fallen asleep. Once through the entrance, his mission was brief and uncomplicated—buy tokens, find a booth, masturbate, leave.

Only later did he happen upon the secrets of the back booths, slowly realizing what other pleasures could be had. But, he also learned, to maintain complete privacy—to avoid trouble, to prevent intrusions—money should get spent; therefore, holding a booth and not paying for a video was forbidden. Furthermore, loitering around the arcade's foyer was reason enough for a patron to be escorted outside, and hanging around Greasewood's parking lot could easily draw the attention of police officers.

For those who needed a crash course, the cardboard sign on the arcade door avoided ambiguity: WANT TO PLAY, YOU GOT TO PAY! THIS ISN'T A FREE RIDE, BOYS AND GIRLS! So as long as a booth remained locked and tokens fed the slot and the television brightly broadcast whatever preference (white, black, Asian, Hispanic, S & M, B & D, well-hung men and tight-assed women fucking nonstop, men sucking men, lesbians with strap-ons, threesomes, foursomes, countless orgies), then the management, as well as the customer, was rarely unhappy. The rules of engagement, the man eventually discerned, were as simple as that.

Now he wonders without conclusion: What kind of man presses his lips against a fist-sized hole? What is the fiber of such a person, or of one who in turn slips his cock through a hole where another man's mouth awaits?

He rubs at his hands, feeling bone, flesh.

He touches his oily forehead, his cold earlobes, his bearded chin.

Then he closes his eyes, returning again: that summer, that arcade, the sounds of pornography behind locked doors (moaning and grunting and Casio-composed music)—those glory holes chiseled between darkly lit booths and unnoticed by him for weeks, ignored until a July afternoon when the rain fell steadily upon the hot streets.

Again he is there, observing himself months ago, seeing himself caught off guard while masturbating inside a booth. Except here, within the tunnel, he is ready for the mouth appearing at the hole; he anticipates the seductive urging: "Hey, bring it here, please let me taste it, bring me your cock."

He remembers being near ejaculation, and, as aroused as he was at that moment, he didn't think twice about acquiescing. No, at that moment it wasn't frightening or creepy, wasn't disgusting letting a faceless mouth give him a blowjob.

So the mouth swallowed him, the tongue zigzagging, the lips sliding along his penis before the shock of orgasm repelled him. Regaining his breath, he spied the mouth's swift vanishing—the lips replaced then by a slender curving erection, dewy with pre-cum, wanting reciprocation, thrusting through the hole; the sight of it churned the man's stomach.

"Suck me," the mouth pleaded.

Zipping his pants, he thought: Stupid, never again.

"Suck me off—"

Turning and rapidly exiting the booth: No more, that's it, you've gone too far.

Yet the experience plagued and aroused him throughout that night, reviving his dormant insomnia. He shifted beneath the sheets, he checked on his children, he went downstairs and watched television, he ate potato chips—all the while contemplating the disquieting eroticism of the mouth and the hole.

The next day, he masturbated feverishly (once in the shower, once in the garage) with the words repeatedly uttered by his own mouth: "Let me taste it—bring me your cock—please let me taste it—" Then whatever guilt he harbored afterwards, whatever reservations remained, dissipated minutes after his family wished him goodnight.

A lifetime is too short for guilt, he reasoned. It's way too brief for token-driven voyeurism, or sex alone in a locked booth. A lifetime, he concluded, should be a curious adventure and worthy of pleasurable risks.

"Keep yourself receptive," he had lectured his students. "Step in different shoes, explore and enjoy, know the rules, and make some of your own—learning is the key to everything, believe me. For those not paying attention, let me say it again—"

Know the rules: locate a back booth with a glory hole, close and lock the door, spend two tokens, begin masturbating as the video plays, wait for someone to whistle or press his lips against the hole (this means he will suck), bring unlubricated condoms (he might not).

"—like I said, learning is the key—"

Make some rules of your own: the man would refuse giving head in return. Also, at least initially, he avoided glimpsing the person sucking him. Attractive, fat, pig faced, skinny, washed, stinky, balding or bald, young or old, short or long haired, faggy or masculine—however they looked and acted was irrelevant (what their mouths and tongues did being his only concern).

"—explore and enjoy—"

But just four booths provided glory holes, and usually they stayed occupied. As a result, he began scanning faces after entering the arcade, seeking eye contact from men leisurely approaching or leaving booths, searching for a lingering glance of interest. When connecting with a suitable someone, preferably his age or younger, he maintained eye contact while stepping into a vacant booth.

Like luring a fish, he imagined. Like hoping for a bite, the bait swallowed.

And with the door unlatched, he unzipped his pants and anticipated the chosen one's inevitably coy entrance.

"Hi—"

"Hi. Come in—"

That general exchange was the overall extent of most of their conversations; little else was spoken outright, the rest getting articulated by a base desire, the rote nature of such transactions (gasps, fluctuations of breath, short and fast thrusts). Yet he felt powerful in those moments, incredibly supreme: he bent for no man, he returned no favors, but they wanted him and needed him and desired him; in those moments he owned them and they always did as he pleased.

He can't recall how many followed, how many gladly dropped to their knees and serviced him (fewer than fifty, more than thirty?); though each man was logged into a notebook, four asterisks marking the memorable encounters, written down for his own fascination, and kept hidden inside his red toolbox:

**** *Native American, long black hair, on his knees licked my balls, quite eager to please me.*

**** *Jockish, late 20s, humped his mouth, gripped his ears, made him choke on it.*

**** *Older, maybe 40s, curious accent, pulled off shirt, wants cum on his chest, no condom, jerked me quick but good, trimmed fingernails.*

**** *Asian, 30s, seen him here before, both just j/o while S & M video shows, sucks me before cumming, nice mouth.*

Not once did he conceive of the trouble his damning entries would bring. Or that those anonymous men, carefully detailed in his own handwriting, would provide further evidence against his innocence, showing him for the pathetic liar that he was. How could he have foreseen his impending plight, the damage of what was written for his own reference? In documenting last summer's diversions, how could he have perceived the unintentional dooming of himself?

"Tobias, do you believe some men are doomed regardless of whether or not they try correcting past mistakes?"

"Well, I'd say we're all doomed. Just seems some are more doomed than some others, don't it?"

Yes, the man thought. Yes.

"Yes," he said.

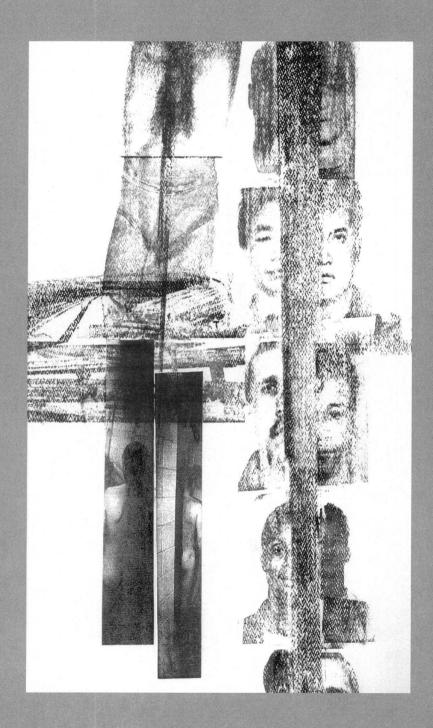

OBSCURED BY darkness, the receptive men of the adult arcades and public toilets drift into a trance fueled by need, into a craving that—as it is satisfied—brings them closer to the perfect lives they dream of, yet are unable to articulate. They kneel before glory holes with their ravenous mouths willing, with enough thirst inside to accept any cock proffered, with caressing fingers to the other's testicles. *Until the bitter end* is their unspoken mantra, invoked through deed, one performing the same as another—the tonguing of an erection and the flavor of the resulting sperm signifies their short-lived nirvana.

Men of all walks seek out this cabalistic pleasure, some openly gay, many more married or recently divorced. The younger ones have begun to abandon the belief in the sacredness of their bodies; those shaped early on by pious parents or by a profound sense of disgust for the sex that governs their primary fantasies. A former college football player forgets his past grandeur on the field, but imagines instead naked teammates sweating in locker rooms. Closeted husbands, insatiable queers, pursuers of hedonism, have accepted the desire, and now return without regrets for what makes them feel utterly alive. The guilt stricken are lulled back by overriding urges which proclaim that, just this once, it's okay to relax and give in again.

Within booths and toilet stalls, these men glimpse a reality they can't readily find elsewhere: agreeable partners and passive strangers, the taste of anonymous skin, identities superseded by like orgasms. There are no selves amongst the lurking men of the adult arcades or public toilets, no assertion of individuality, no hint of personal history or accomplishment or value existing beyond the booths and stalls. Those who have embraced their desperation—the homosexuals, the lonely men—sometimes hope they will change, they will find real love, they will settle down and finally resist the pull into darker places. Others think nothing of the sort, remaining quite gratified with servicing strangers and being serviced by them; the darker places, they know, are exactly where they should be.

In the man's case, he has no affinity for such men, nor does he consider his previous longings as somehow truly homosexual, though he doesn't believe homosexuality is a biological error or indecent or sinful. For him, same-sex attraction is simply a lifestyle contrary to his understanding of himself. Certainly he has enjoyed sexual activity with a diverse number of those men, the majority of which were probably gay, but his affections are reserved for women (particularly his wife Julie, who he now misses more than he ever imagined possible).

So the separation he makes is not complex: I love Julie, I could never love a man like I love her. Sex and love, he has reasoned, are two separate things—a distinction should always be drawn between loving another male and receiving a blowjob from another man's lips; he refuses to view it any other way.

Moreover, the male form rarely arouses him; to his mind, a penis isn't nearly as enjoyable and interesting as a vagina and breasts, the folds and curves of a female's body. When alone in a booth, his videos of choice usually featured a man and a woman having sex—maybe two women by themselves, on occasion two men and a woman.

While sharing a booth with someone else, the gay hardcore was viewed for their benefit and never for his; it was a courtesy he hardly begrudged—if the person sucking him was properly stimulated, then he was properly stimulated.

After all, he figured, homosexuals had it difficult enough without having straight porn forced on them as they gave head. And, being as accommodating as possible, the man at least wanted whoever was servicing him to think their needs were important too—even if it meant watching two men fuck beside a swimming pool.

"Homosexuals are humans like you and me," he once told a student who grumbled about Whitman's poetry seeming *faggy.* "Their blood is red, their tears are exactly like yours."

"Yeah, but how come we have to hear about them? I mean, come on, what a guy does with a guy is his business—but keep it to yourself because it's like gross, you know?"

"I think you're missing the point."

The point is always missed, he thinks now. Love is love, sex is sex—the end result of these things is what's important: how we show our love, how we give of ourselves through sex. So the point is invariably missed every day—in schools, in offices, especially in churches.

"What point? Mr. Connor, God made Adam and Eve—not Adam and Steve."

Adam and Eve, not Adam and Steve: the man recalls first hearing the tired joke six years ago, spoken slyly among husbands in the parking lot of Desert Baptist Oasis. He had followed the group outside, leaning quietly against a tailgate while the wives continued inside the church with the Wednesday evening *Bible* study and couples' seminar (the men taking a brief leave to sip coffee and share their brotherhood). But the brotherhood was an exclusive bunch, the man soon realized. A white Christian brotherhood born of implicit beliefs: to merely stand beside them was to suggest a like-mindedness—no liberalism, no welfare concern, no sympathy for queers or illegal immigrants.

Christian men shaking their heads when someone mentioned the disease of National Coming Out Day, frowning at the idea of a Million Mom march on Washington. Then they would laugh, the brotherhood would exchange jokes—*it's not Adam and Steve*—and glibly say *faggots* and *queers* over the rims of Styrofoam cups.

A dozen so-called Christians, the man thought. UnChristlike good ol' boy husbands with contemptuous wives.

Even Julie, who generally feared homosexuals, was bothered when he mentioned what was said in the parking lot: "It's not nice, you know, those guys saying that—and at the church. Aren't we supposed to forgive the sinners but hate the sins, right? That's how it is."

This was before she gained weight and the embarrassment of her body stopped her from attending Wednesday meetings, before her strong thighs became flabby, her once long face turned oval and puffy. Without ever expressing it, he was delighted she no longer felt comfortable going, was relieved to be freed from associating with such hypocrites.

"Pharisaical fools," he imagined calling them; how he regretted sipping coffee and keeping silent, listening as some jackass went on and on about Christ's infinite love and forgiveness.

Or perhaps he could have changed their minds, perhaps he might have offered intelligent opinions and thoughts regarding homosexuals (opinions his own wife had never heard from him): for he has admired gays; they are often creative and sweet people, they scarcely bring impoverished children into this mutable and overpopulated world, they are neat, clean, they give great head. As a teacher, he had students who were clearly gay (maybe they weren't aware of it yet, maybe they were struggling with it), most of whom were hardworking, fastidious, and decent. They are symbols, he imagines, of the complexity of love, examples of God's mysterious ways.

Yet he remembers Julie adamantly explaining that gay men must seduce boys into their ranks. "Keeps their movement going," she told him. "That's why we've got so many these days."

Debating the issue proved pointless. She had already heard the sordid details of what had occurred when he was fifteen: in the showers at the municipal swimming pool, a stranger bathing nearby, a middle-aged man, lathered his penis and then began masturbating.

"You poor thing," his wife said after he related the story. "How awful. He could've raped you, or worse. Did you report him or get help?"

"No, I was too shocked and no one else was around, just me and him. I couldn't believe it—so I left the showers and went home. Didn't figure it was a big deal, just weird. You're the only person I've ever told."

"That's horrendous, really disgusting. You know, a lot of men are really creepy—you'd be surprised—most men really are pigs, it's true."

How often had she said that? How often had he heard from her and several women he worked with about the weak qualities of men? Never once had he told them that men deserve much more credit than the current vogue of dismissing innate male behavior (which, in his mind, was simply masking a larger contempt for men in general). Never had he said that men should be praised instead for functioning while enslaved by such crippling impulses and desires.

It's a miracle, he has thought, that men accomplish anything profound—especially when considering the nature of their sex drive. It's a miracle that they built roads and formed societies and wrote books and articulated intelligent thoughts.

In truth, he believed, the best of men have always been noble, and most men have strived to be greater than their overpowering genetic dispositions; even so, few men are capable of fully rising above it—and that must be accepted without complete scorn. For all he or Julie knew, the middle-aged man in the shower might have done more good than they ever had.

"Still, you're lucky he didn't touch you. He probably wanted to."

"Well, he didn't—I never gave him the chance."

"Good," she said. "You should have reported him, though."

"Yeah, I should have."

Except, of course, she couldn't know he followed suit, also jerking off in the steam and warm running water—the two of them facing each other, saying nothing; both ejaculating seconds apart, the stranger's sperm running thick and milky around his curled fingertips.

Thereafter, he went from the showers, promptly dressed, and headed home—the encounter leaving him completely untainted (his well-imagined masturbatory fantasies involving Marsha Brady and Grace Slick weren't then deposed by erotic musings of a naked David Cassidy or Mick Jagger). In fact, the stranger's face became impossible; he couldn't say if the middle-aged man had dark or blond or sandy hair, if his body was lean or stocky or average. He only recollected the risk of the moment, the sheer thrill of taking part in something considered filthy and sick and likely evil—and that notion was potent enough to make the boy he once was reach down past the band of his jockey shorts, blissfully.

What a good-looking boy he was then, almost pretty—very slender with puppy dog eyes, full lips—one worthy of being sought after by suspect men who desired teenagers. But the shower incident notwithstanding, he avoided any real sexual contact until meeting Julie in college (a blind date, arranged casually by a mutual friend). And as clichéd as it sounded, he honestly believed that theirs was a love at first sight. She was a virgin from Mesa—a devout Christian, intense, shy, loved *Star Trek*, snorted as she chuckled, thin and blond, charming, moody, getting her degree in Health and Human Performance; he was a virgin from Phoenix—a fast talker, feeling suave in granny glasses and bell-bottoms, an English student infatuated with Beckett's early novels.

They finally married during their senior year, honeymooned at Puerto La Cruz, and soon settled into domesticity (him teaching English, she instructing jazzercise). By the time David arrived, the man's thick hair had thinned, his stomach had lost most of its firmness.

Then Monica came along (they wanted two), and Julie changed, growing disinterested and chubby—no more church meetings, no more jazzercise, no more sex on Saturday mornings; instead, solitary walks pushing a baby stroller, some gardening, and kind admonishments as he anxiously grabbed for her breasts.

"Will you stop it—"

"Oh, come on—let me suckle you."

"Try suckling yourself, I'm beat."

Not that their physical needs were mutual, or their congress ever prolific (their sex life diminishing drastically with David's birth), but twice a month, he figured, would have been sufficient.

So justifications were easily found regarding his summer visits to the arcade, few misgivings were shouldered for what he did there and later at Mission Park. In an effort to minimize his guilt, he convinced himself that Julie wouldn't really mind his kind of philandering; she denied sex, for him it was essential and healthy—and as long as he was safe, as long as he didn't dare cheat with a woman, then their marriage would remain unscathed.

Now everything is in disrepair: Julie has left him, taking David and Monica with her; his house is no longer his home and he lives underground. Then how far away the monsoon season seems, how alien that thunder and fast-falling rain and humidity and golf courses wet like marshlands.

He mulls that past, turning it over in his head, forming

a circle which continually brings him to the same place: If I'd made myself content at the arcade, if the familiar faces and glory holes hadn't grown monotonous, I wouldn't have gone to the Mission Park toilet. If I'd just made myself content at the arcade—if my curiosity hadn't gotten the best of me—

But all it took was one mouth speaking from a glory hole, saying to him, "I took your cock two weeks ago, right? At Mission Park, Wednesday afternoon in the bathroom near the baseball field—it was you, right? Inside the back stall—ring a bell? Remember me, remember how we did it?"

"Yes," the man replied, pushing his cock through the hole and into the mouth. "Show me again. Show me how you did it—"

Nevertheless, it wasn't him the mouth was talking about; the man had yet to discover the poorly lit men's toilet, or the protocol involved (enter the stall at the far end, shut the door, sit and wait, start tapping both feet after someone steps into the adjacent stall—when interest is stirred, the person within the adjacent stall will either kneel and say something or leave to discreetly join you). The rules of Mission Park, however, would become familiar shortly, as would the foul lingering of human waste. The cause for retreat from Greasewood happening twofold: on a stormy evening he passed a recently graduated student while entering the arcade; their eyes locked in the foyer and unnerved him.

"Hey, Mr. Connor, what's up?"

"Hello, James."

"Weird seeing you here."

"I suppose so—"

Then claiming a back booth by himself, he noticed the glory hole had been sealed, covered with a square metal sheet and bolted. At that moment the adult arcade lost his patronage altogether. He wasted not a second in exiting, moving swiftly through the shop and out the door, pulling his jacket over his head as he crossed the parking lot—where the rain thumped against him, the wind rustled his clothing; that very wind then pushed his Suburban along the highway, taking him farther from home—delivering him to Mission Park and the public toilet, to a damp stall which felt more provocative than the relative safety of the back booths. And he wasn't alone there—others were waiting, at least three, occupying nearby stalls, tapping feet.

New faces, new bodies, new mouths.

He would leave minutes later, tired and ready for bed.

The next day he would return.

Like magic, he thought, crawling into bed. Like heaven.

The rain hit the guest bedroom windows, calming and steady.

Then he ebbed from his surroundings and slept, but not before revisiting the toilet briefly—the urinals visible even in darkness, the stall door swinging inward, the ghost-like shape of someone reaching for him, whispering, "Yes—"

Like magic: he would go tomorrow, he would return.

Like heaven.

Except soon he realized the public toilet offered less variety, often the action was non-existent (he'd wait at the urinals in vain, hoping for someone to stand beside him—someone he could then lure into the back stall). Even so, the atmosphere couldn't be better—the shouts of kids playing baseball outside, footsteps echoing across the concrete floor, the whooshing of running urinals—each enhancing the risky activity going on within the stalls, the moans and muted acclamations.

There he could receive a blowjob, shutting his eyes and breathing deeply while others obliviously washed their hands at the sink; in time he would end up fucking someone as basketball-playing teenagers urinated several feet away: "Dude, I rocked—did you see it? I swatted his ass, you saw it." He slid into another, conjoining with one who had started servicing him on Thursday and Saturday evenings. Polo, the man called him—because of the cologne the guy sometimes wore, because the man didn't know his real name.

Polo: describing himself as a passive bottom—"but no barebacking, condoms a must"—and from the gold band on his ring finger the man gathered that their situations were comparable.

"Gentle, don't go too fast."

The man standing behind Polo.

Polo bending, his hands flattening on the toilet seat.

"Okay, tell me if it hurts."

"It doesn't—it feels great, go slow—"

How their bodies began operating in accord, how singular the man felt then—pushing inside Polo, drawing out, pushing inside. No glory hole mouth had been so velvety and tight and warm; he had never ejaculated so intensely as he did when finishing inside Polo.

"Oh fuck," the man stammered, "oh god—"

Afterwards Polo turned to him, putting his lips near the man's ear. "Thank you," he said. "You were awesome."

"So were you."

"Thank you."

Nothing was expected in return; Polo wanted only to please, to suck or get fucked. This disposition, along with his weekly reliability (he would always be there on time, he would wait if necessary), engendered a fondness toward him from the man, who was always glad when spotting him loitering within the park toilet, standing patiently beside a urinal. Often Polo was found inside the back stall—though at times the man wasn't sure if it was actually him lurking there in the shadows (the differences between one partner and another blurred in the predictability of each encounter). It also didn't hurt that, even while obscured mostly by darkness, he could tell Polo was handsome, around the man's age but fit, his short hair and wide eyes giving him a younger look (nicely dressed, sharp in tan Dockers, a button-down shirt), and, immediately after sex, his habit of kissing the man's neck displayed a tenderness which put the arcade men in sharp contrast.

"Was it good?"

"Very."

Then the kiss, moist lips against the man's throat.

"I'll see you Saturday?"

"Yes. I might be a little later than usual."

Another kiss.

"That's fine, I'll wait, whenever."

What the man regrets now is that he avoided asking Polo his name, that he expressed no interest in his job or life. He never invited him for a beer, never sat down with him and said, "Tell me about yourself. Do you have children?"

And if everything hadn't concluded so badly, he might better relish the memories of those Mission Park evenings with him—the fragrance of Polo revealing his presence inside the stall, then him wanting fingers slipped into his mouth as the man slid into him from behind, the rain and thunder obscuring the clamor of their copulation. Or, in particular, that bright night when they met in front of the public toilet and observed three police cars parked several yards away: "Let's go somewhere else," Polo suggested. "Somewhere private."

"I know a place, it's perfect."

So together they went, Polo riding shotgun in the man's Suburban—cruising with open windows, speeding toward the Tucson mountains, eventually finding themselves miles from the public toilet and parked at the far end of the overlook.

Then how beautiful it was seeing the stars glimmering high above, how pleasant and relaxed, the entire city spread below—and later, while returning home exhausted, how sorry the man felt for having had Polo's intimacy there, the two of them embracing in the front seat before sex, talking for a while like lovers about the stars and an unfathomable universe.

"Amazing, all that space and darkness and we're floating in it."

"It's beautiful, it's so clear tonight."

"I know, isn't it?"

"I love it up here."

"Me too."

"I love being here with you."

"Me too."

But it should've been Julie, he thinks now. It should've been her—her and me, never anyone else—it should've always been her—

IN TOBIAS' dream the man was running uphill, at night, near a remote town (from the adobe houses and low-lying mountains Tobias figured the community must exist somewhere in the high desert Southwest). Short of breath, he continued onward, jogging toward a solitary cabin found at the end of a dirt cul-de-sac—beyond which stretched a shadowy plain of pinyon trees and creosote bushes.

"Buddy, you was spooked shitless—you was goin' as hurried as possible 'cept it's winter and colder than a witch's tit—and your warm air chugged out like car smoke—no tellin' what was behind you, too dark—but you'd turn and look back, turn and look back—maybe somethin' there snappin' at yer heels, couldn't say fer sure—and lackin' jacket or shoes as well, shiverin' and shakin' and teeth chatterin', you'd best get on into that cabin—better get on inside 'cause it was all lit, safe and warm—you knew it."

Then there was Tobias' other dream, the one he revealed last week, relating the details as they foraged for kindling.

"Strangest of things, there you was stuffin' grass in yer mouth, chompin' it like a horse eatin' cud, lips gone green from the stuff—and I says to you, Buddy, why ya eatin' all that grass? And you go, It's my fuel, need it for flyin'. So I says, Need it for flyin'? And you nod, sayin' nothin' else 'cause yer already chompin' more grass. 'Fore I knows it, there you go—flyin' off into the sky, flappin' yer arms same as a bird, shootin' up, soarin' around. Buddy, I yells, when ya comin' down? 'Cept by then you was already far off, a lil' dot to my eyes. Ain't that somethin', I was thinkin', ain't ol' buddy a hoot."

The substance of those dreams is disquieting, though the man tries not to dwell on them. Instead, he reminds himself that Tobias knows him only as buddy, a fellow vagrant first encountered while wandering Papago Park (Tobias has never asked his real name, the man has never spoken it). On the nights they stay awake talking, Tobias has shown no interest in the man's past, hasn't wondered about his circumstances; the man always extends the same courtesy.

Yet without any knowledge of who buddy really is or what has befallen him, the revelations of Tobias' two dreams—both vague in meaning, open to interpretation—seized the man with an uneasy familiarity: eating grass for flight fuel is absurd, but he did mow lawns as a boy, working weekends so he could buy model airplane kits, sometimes hoarding lunch money in order to hasten the purchase of a Corsair F4U or a Gee Bee Racer or a T33 Jet Trainer. He and his father built them together, spending hours in the work shed assembling models which would soon hang from the mobiles in his bedroom (clear plastic thread for the vertical hangers, wire flexible enough to bend for the crossarms).

"The airport," he called that bedroom. "My airport."

It was his father who instilled in him a passion for flight, teaching him how to erect airplanes and fashion the mobiles from which they hung—such a patient and gentle person, much older than other fathers with boys the same age: sixty-two, a retired Air Force captain with a twelve-year-old son.

"You're a miracle," his father often said. "You came late to my game, and I'm thankful."

Late to both his parents' game (he was their second child, born two days before their first child, a daughter, turned fourteen). When the man was twelve, his sister was twenty-five—so age kept them too far apart for any real sense of kinship to develop; she married as he attended grade school, she moved to Chicago as he started junior high, after their father died they rarely kept in touch. Christmas cards. Birthday cards. Phone conversations regarding their mother's assisted living at a retirement home. And while he gained no pleasure in thinking so, the man believed his father favored him over his sister. Or perhaps, because his father had mellowed with age, he reaped the benefits of maturation; apparently, as a younger man, his father had been quite temperamental and discipli-nary minded, whereas the man only knew the softer side of him: the benign gray eyes, the ambling gait, the bald head and white mustache. Then there were his father's hands (nimble and tender and always lotioned) putting his son to sleep at night, rubbing the boy's neck and back; his very touch meant safety, each caress a reassurance and an accept-ance.

Now the man questions if he could have ever expected his father to die so abruptly, to simply grasp his chest with those comforting hands and collapse on the work shed floor without saying goodbye. Could he have imagined the long nights afterwards, wide awake in his bedroom but feigning drowsiness, listening as his mother read aloud—*David Copperfield* or *Gone With The Wind* or sometimes the pages of greeting card sentiments she wrote as a hobby.

As you go through life's trials
remember the beauty of each day
and the lives you touch
with your steady presence...

THANK YOU FOR BEING YOU

Then he would eventually begin yawning and, as if on cue, his mother would kiss him goodnight. She would tell him to sleep well, turning out the bedroom light before leaving.

"Sweet dreams—see you in the morning."

But even when he was a boy sleep was elusive, failing to absorb him until he routinely stood upon his bed and touched the wings of favorite planes; at that age it was so easy to imagine himself sailing among clouds, flying in tandem with the rewards of his and his father's labor, his sleek body an F-14A Tomcat. He's wondered how much grass it took to bring him there, to give his mind flight. Tons, he assumes now, a whole childhood's worth.

Nevertheless, it was Tobias' initial dream that nearly panicked the man, and once it was described—the high desert town, the running, the cabin—they sat silently beside the fire, sipping coffee as wood crackled. Perhaps Tobias saw then the shock on the man's face, perhaps it was the frightened look in his eyes that made the old vagrant continue. "Not worth puttin' stock in, buddy—'cause normally I'm takin' part in my fancies, kinda part of the situations—'cept you was there runnin' all by yourself, tryin' your damnedest to get to that cabin. Sure enough I was seein' it all, but more like it was watchin' a movie and I gots no idea what's goin' on—I mean, there you is, all chilly and cold, huffin' along, scared outta yer wits, and I'm wonderin' afters I wake up, how come he don't got a jacket on? Where's he comin' from that he ain't got no time to put shoes on his feet?"

Just coincidence, the man concluded at the time. Uncanny, close to the money, but coincidence without question.

"Hell, buddy, it ain't nothin'—don't mean a thing, don't know why I bothered tellin' you."

Still, almost three months ago the man did flee something horrific, speeding breathlessly toward the safety of his home, his agitated gaze studying the rearview in case he was being followed. It's also true that his blue windbreaker got tossed into a dumpster along the way, leaving him jacketless on a rainy night. Aside from those vexing similarities, little else matched Tobias' dream—the incident had occurred at Mission Park and not somewhere in the high desert; he wore sneakers, his escape wasn't on foot; his house wasn't a cabin.

So after they finished their coffee and had talked of other things (coyote mating rituals, how raw garlic can keep mosquitoes off skin, the morning Tobias accidentally stepped on a diamondback's head), the man pushed inside his sleeping bag, resisting the grave feelings churning his stomach. He tried envisioning happier days: afternoons working alone in his garden, the summer he and Julie hiked the north rim of the Grand Canyon, the delight spreading across David's face when he deftly maneuvered their remote-operated Mark II Lysander free of a tailspin.

But ultimately the good memories weren't strong enough, and, shutting his eyes, breathing smoke from the fire, he returned again to the Mission Park toilet, entering the place on that fateful night, where a mighty breeze howled through the open doorway and the fragrance of Polo cologne sent him sailing into the back stall.

The man shifts within his sleeping bag, crossing his arms on his chest.

Any given life can change on a dime, he thinks, while considering how indifferently, how carelessly most people go about their days—the driver fiddling with the radio dial seconds before the collision, the mother pestering a child to hurry off to school and never seeing him or her again, the rapturous orgasm spurting infectious seed into an unsuspecting body. Like a kiss which, as it is bestowed upon a loved one, isn't seen for what it will inevitably become—the finishing kiss, the last pressing of those particular lips.

Like the final night he drove across the city to visit Mission Park, stopping briefly at Albertson's to buy lubricated condoms before cruising along the streets and avenues, momentarily traveling beneath the interstate bridge—radio tuned to an oldies station, both hands gripping the steering wheel—past the seemingly endless construction sites whose sameness had occasionally confused him, so that he sometimes mistakenly zoomed beyond the park entrance (located obscurely between the forthcoming Vista Loma Estates and Quail Run Village). On that blustery night, however, he would get it right; he would make the correct turn, he would find himself there again—exiting his Suburban, walking briskly toward the public toilet building, yet hampered by that wind which followed him from his car to the building's entrance.

Even as he has repeatedly probed his memory, the man doesn't remember seeing anyone else loitering nearby when he entered the building. Though during previous visits, he recalls well enough, someone was invariably lingering outside or standing at a urinal—but because he wasn't cruising for new action that night, because he knew who waited for him in the back stall (Polo's Dockers already pushed to his knees, his erection burgeoning amidst neatly trimmed pubic hairs), the man went forward without searching the shadows (hands within his windbreaker pockets, fingers wrapped around the condom pack), eagerly anticipating their sex—the whispered hellos, Polo unzipping the man's pants and then sucking him until the penis was properly erect for a condom; Polo pivoting and bending over, hands flattened against the toilet seat, exhaling with gratification as the man pressed slowly into his anus.

Except that night it would be different: they barely had time to exchange greetings before the groans of other men caught their attention—then both paused, shoulders touching, listening as low grunts and fervid utterances grew louder beside the urinals.

Two men struggling toward orgasm, the man imagined. Two strangers with their pants surely unbuckled, apparently fucking in plain sight, shunning even a minimal amount of discretion.

He squeezed Polo's wrist and smiled through the darkness: "Damn—"

"Sounds hot," Polo muttered, his breath warm against the man's chin.

Neither could have anticipated the deafening pop which

suddenly resonated throughout the building, stunning their ears—or the accompanying silver-white burst, like a flash-tube's momentary eruption, that briefly illuminated the ceiling.

Soon they both would leave the stall (Polo, who nearly fell while pulling up his pants, fled without saying anything; the man, following reluctantly seconds thereafter, walked haltingly forward). But first they would remain hidden within the stall for a while, frightened and uncertain, their ringing ears gradually attuning to the abrupt quiet around them—no more groans, no second pop, just the wind's brisk humming beyond the doorway. Regardless, they didn't move, didn't dare shift a foot—not until a motorcycle broke the silence, its engine grumbling fiercely as the vehicle sped from the parking lot. Then, without waiting, Polo bolted; his swift departure was marked by an agonized mumble, a breathless voice faltering near the urinals: "Oh fuck—please—someone—fuck—"

In hindsight, the man knows he shouldn't have walked cautiously from the stall, pursuing the plea for help. No, he should've run from the restroom like Polo had and never looked back. Instead, he found himself crouched beside a corpse—a young black man whose head rested at the mouth of a urinal, whose hands still clutched his own neck, whose fingers and hands were glazed with blood (all that blood, so much of it, bubbling profusely from a wound under his left earlobe, making a puddle on the floor and seeping into drains).

And—the man has since convinced himself—had the body twitched, had the lips attempted another word, he would have certainly seized the pay phone outside and dialed 911. However, the victim's pallid gaze urged the man to do otherwise—those vacant eyes somehow imploring him to leave, to go in case the attacker might return or, worse, his reasons for being there might become known: the man hurried past the doorway, zipping his windbreaker as he sprinted across the parking lot. Absently digging for his keys, he searched for Polo, but saw nothing other than his Suburban surrounded by empty parking spaces. The wind ruffled his windbreaker—the wind shook trees and lifted trash from trashcans, doing so with a lamenting, ceaseless sigh.

Perhaps I was in shock, the man thinks now while trying to comprehend what, if anything, he felt when unlocking his car (someone was murdered, someone spoke their last words, but the entire tragedy seemed oddly mundane). Minutes later though, during the drive home, the horror finally took root—his hands started trembling as he glanced occasionally in the rearview mirror (no vehicle followed, no motorcycle tailgated the Suburban); soon his vision blurred with tears. Then waiting at a red light, he noticed blood on a jacket sleeve, and this discovery incited powerful spasms in his chest, producing crippling sobs which made it almost impossible to proceed any further: "Jesus—oh Jesus Christ—"

Could've been me, he thought after disposing of the jacket in an alley dumpster. Could've been me, he thought after arriving home, relieved to be parked safely in the driveway.

Could've been me—

The wind, he suspects, eventually calmed him—the whistling around the Suburban, steady and rhythmic, in a way tranquil. It was the wind reviving him and clearing his mind as he stepped from the vehicle—the wind carrying him to the front porch, sending him indoors.

Inside, Julie watched Action 7 News on the living room couch, relaxing in her baby blue housecoat, smiling at the sight of him reflected upon the television screen, yet furrowing her brow when glancing over a shoulder and spotting him there: "Where's your windbreaker?"

Where's my windbreaker?

He didn't stammer, his expression didn't convey fear. Then it was as if his mouth began functioning independently of his brain.

He thought: Julie, a man was murdered tonight.

He said, "Left it at the library."

"You did? Where?"

"On a chair, I think, or underneath my reading table."

"You didn't go back for it?"

No, he hadn't gone back for it. He had been reading at his favorite table on the third floor, absorbed in a book about kamikaze pilots, when the library's closing was announced—so he headed downstairs, failing to realize his jacket was left behind until entering the chill of the parking garage.

"I'll get it first thing tomorrow. I'm sure it's safe."

"Better be," she said. "My mother gave you that windbreaker."

The windbreaker was unimportant, meaningless. The next day he would return to the library and find it gone, or at least he would tell her that. What really mattered to him then was Julie—he kissed her forehead, stroked her hair. He asked if the children were sleeping.

"Yes, of course they are."

He asked if she still loved him.

"Yes, what a dumb question."

He stretched out on the couch, resting his head in her lap. He stared up at her face and asked if she was happy.

"Pretty much," she said, bending to kiss his lips.

He closed his eyes, and sensed the persistent trembling of his hands.

"You're cold," she said. "Let me warm you."

She kissed him again, cradling his head against her belly.

Home, he thought. I'm home.

IT IS an itinerant wind blowing into the tunnel, enlivening camp fire cinders, which again revives fragments of the man's past; this abrupt desert tempest—charging down the arroyo as if accompanying fast-flowing water, whistling harmonically through the tunnel's circuitous entrance, stirring up random memories like bits of torn newspaper: nine years old and on a hunting trip with his father, roughing it deep within New Mexican wilderness (a breeze rustling their tent late one night, keeping him awake as his father slept soundly nearby); the brisk fall afternoon when he asked Julie to marry him, the pair hugging while golden leaves drifted off campus trees and floated around them; thorny ocotillo branches swaying in the backyard during his son's first birthday, hinting at the sandstorm which would soon arrive and send partygoers fleeing indoors; the five wind chimes hanging from the front porch awning, tinkling a faint yet soothing cacophony as he napped inside with his newborn daughter; a vast blue sky above the overlook parking lot, where the box kite he was flying faltered and careened toward the earth, dully hitting the asphalt.

Then—despite the vigor with which it came—the wind at once ceases altogether, leaving the man plagued by a solitary image that won't disappear (even as his eyes remain open, even as he gazes at the cinders and watches the orangish glow fade without the wind's encouragement); in his mind, there are two lifeless pupils staring up at him, two dead eyes delivering judgment—and there is blood—and there is that breeze touching everything just beyond the doorway of the Mission Park toilet.

"Ronald Jerome Banister," the man says, whispering the name.

Two brown eyes, fingers curled around the neck, the blood puddling upon the cold concrete floor—all belonging to Ronald Jerome Banister.

Some names are easily forgotten, he has thought.

Other names, for whatever reasons, roll about the brain like a mouthful of marbles (but how could he ever forget this one?). From reading the obituary and countless newspaper articles, from watching local news broadcasts, the victim had eventually become more familiar to the man than any of those he encountered within the toilet or at the arcade.

"I know you," he utters, nudging the cinders with an empty Coors can, "and you know nothing of me."

Ronald—Jerome—Banister: born in Phoenix, murdered at twenty-nine, attended Arizona State University on a track and field scholarship, married Angela Hidalgo (an attorney specializing in environmental issues), father of two young sons (Ronald Jr. and Jerome), hobbies included lifting weights, touch football, restoring vintage cars, playing bass in an R & B band called The Third Degree; as a decorated law enforcer, he was apparently beloved by many, including a few he had arrested—and last August someone shot him with his own gun, killing him inside a public toilet rumored to be a hotbed of illicit activity.

But Ronald Jerome Banister died in the line of duty; the papers stated this fact repeatedly; he was posing undercover, loitering beside the urinals until an indecent proposition or unquestionable grope could be offered (numerous complaints had already been filed—the papers also reported—claiming that blatant and lewd sexual behavior made the toilet unsafe for both Little Leaguers and adults, thus tarnishing the park's once solid reputation as a *positive family environment*). Furthermore, he wasn't alone while operating undercover—his partner roamed on the other side of the park when the shooting occurred, strolling between mesquite trees with a flashlight, searching picnic tables and benches on that windy night (the flashlight encountering nothing criminal until its beam finally found Banister's body).

Later his partner appeared inconsolable, fighting back tears during a press conference, explaining, "Didn't hear anything—the weather functioned as a major problem—just a real obstacle—so if anyone knows anything or saw anything or heard anything that night, I pray they'll please step forward, do the right thing—Ron was a great guy, a good father, he was my friend."

Soon afterwards—as if prompted solely by the murder— came the Week Without Violence, in which Banister's wife and sons led a procession through downtown, holding hands, wearing white T-shirts emblazoned with his face; his oldest boy, Ronald Jr., paused long enough to address a news affiliate's microphone, speaking nervously as marchers moved around him: "Whoever took my father—killed him—I want them to know they shot my dad and I can't see him no more—not ever—and the violence should stop so other kids won't lose their dads or moms or friends or whatever— because it's wrong—killing is wrong—"

There were candlelight vigils.

There were minutes of silence.

There were songs of tribute sung by crowds gathered at Mission Park—not just for the slain police officer, but for the countless others who had met violent deaths elsewhere (*let no one be left behind, let no one be forsaken, let no one fall without purpose*—). There were interviews with friends and associates, human interest articles designed to show Banister as a vibrant figure rather than a murder victim (photographs of him as a smiling child, high school yearbook pictures, videotape footage of him sprinting in a college track event and of him, as a laughing young father, hoisting his son up to his broad shoulders on Christmas morning).

Then there was the short poem the officer wrote in sixth grade for his mother, made more poignant by Ronald Jr.'s emotional reading of it at the conclusion of the candlelight vigil.

The sky has clouds of many shapes
And some look like they are whales
And some look like they have tails
And some look like little tiny snails
But every cloud is special and rare
Giving hope when no hope is here

Several journalists, who first began covering the story as a tragedy, ultimately revised their accounts into like eulogies of bravery and heroic sacrifice: *He was always aware of the risks, the possible dangers, but Ronald Jerome Banister was undaunted by fear. To his wife he often said, "If anything happens to me while I'm working, remember I was doing what I love doing most." Today she finds comfort from his words. So while she must endure the pain of losing a husband and the father of her two children, she also knows that the high price he paid for serving and protecting our community will never be forgotten.*

In the days following the murder, the man saved every newspaper containing an account, piling a neat stack by the garage door (the dailies arranged chronologically and by edition). He caught the *Action 9* news broadcasts—six a.m., noon, five p.m., ten p.m. (usually videotaping channel 4's news program at the same time).

But what he learned was what he had already assumed on his own: the authorities believed Banister had been approached by someone for sex, most likely a male suspect; when the officer attempted to arrest the individual a brief scuffle ensued, and Banister's gun was drawn, somehow finding its way into the wrong hands: a single bullet discharged, striking the officer's head. The gun, a snub-nosed revolver, either fell or was deliberately discarded in a urinal (the chlorine tab and running water removing all fingerprints).

Sequestered at his worktable, the man eventually began gluing each Banister-related article within the pages of his toolbox notebook. Then in the margins, just as was done with his students' essays, he went about correcting the mistakes reported by journalists (the red ink of his pen visible near the repeated statements that Banister died instantly, without any suffering—a slight falsehood which, he understood, probably brought the grieving wife and sons a degree of solace). Now he wishes his intentions for creating the scrapbook had been more honorable; that—when the killer was apprehended, when suspicion couldn't somehow get cast in his direction—he had planned to anonymously send the notebook to investigators, thereby aiding a conviction.

However, the thought never crossed his mind—probably because he was certain the killer's arrest would become an ironclad affair. And, regardless of how he has tried to justify it, the man knows the scrapbook was kept for his own perusal, nothing more—just as he had meticulously fashioned other such records over the years (a stamp collection, drawings of favorite airplanes, binders containing copies of J.D. Salinger's uncollected short stories, magazine photographs of Audrey Hepburn, a journal chronicling hiking trips with Julie, David's and Monica's evolving handprints, his favorite student essays, the descriptions of men he had met at Greasewood Palace and Mission Park).

Soon, he believed, the killer's face and name would be added to the notebook pages.

Soon, he was convinced, the newspapers would proclaim an arrest. Then his guilt for having kept quiet would lessen considerably.

Yet after weeks of anticipation, not a single suspect emerged, no information was offered, no leads given—and while taking care of chores around the house or eating meals with his family, his thoughts suddenly turned vexing, his nights became sleepless again. Only then—watering his garden, eating potato salad, sitting wide awake before the television—did he fully comprehend that something evil had visited Mission Park, something unholy and repugnant. He had, for the first time, shared death's proximity and inhaled its breath, unwittingly binding his secrets to a darker truth: he might spend a lifetime harboring what he knew about Banister's killing; his own misdemeanors might prevent him from righting a great misdeed.

"Can you pass the peas?"

"Yes."

"Do you want more tea?"

"I'm good. Thanks."

Naturally, he now avoided the Mission Park toilet, and pretended the Greasewood Adult Shop never existed while driving past its location. In fact, the very idea of revisiting those places caused tremendous anxiety (his hands trembled slightly, sometimes bile filled his throat).

By summer's end, he attempted masturbating with his old stash of pornography—a tattered *Playboy*, a ragged *Hustler*—trying unsuccessfully to block the glory holes, the open mouths and fervent tongues, and Polo's warm body from memory. Except his orgasms were weak, impotent—the sperm dribbling over his fingers as Banister's voice called out for help.

So, in a way, he was grateful for the lack of sleep, feeling certain that the dead officer would manifest the second he drifted off, aiming a finger at him: "You chicken-shit! You didn't help me, you left me there and drove home!"

Then how jittery he felt while working the garden, how distracted and nervous when playing catch with David—if

72

a car door slammed he jumped, if thunder cracked he covered his ears and went inside.

Somewhere in this city, he thought again and again, there is a man who killed a police officer; there is a murderer living on a street like mine and who, chances are, has seen me in the toilet—who has possibly held my cock in his hand.

Two or three times a week, at dusk, the man still finds himself climbing from the arroyo to cross Papago Park and sit beside the duck pond. While there he has contemplated Ronald Jerome Banister's killer, attempting to gain some needed insight on the person who unwittingly orchestrated his downfall. But, regardless of how he has tried forming a specific composite, what is known of the killer is simply this: male, rides a motorcycle, strong enough to wrestle a gun away from a weight-lifting cop, clearly lives a life of secrets and lies and deception. Then whatever the man chooses to believe about the killer becomes purely speculation: perhaps married with children, perhaps a hobbyist with an avid passion for motorcycles, perhaps carries the burden of his crime without showing outward signs of distress; the guilt is surely justified, the reasoning done while tuning up motorcycles inside the garage—*I have a family, I have a job, I had to protect myself and everything that is dear to me, everything I have loved and worked for—what else could I do?*

You could've called the police and apologized, the man has wanted to yell in the killer's opaque face. Or you could've written an anonymous letter and offered your regrets to the family. You could've made it clear that you and Banister weren't the only people in the toilet that night, that at least two others were there and heard the scuffle. You could've considered other men like yourself—those of us who go where you go and do what you enjoy doing. You could've saved me. You could've—

In the end, however, the man settles on a single immutable truth: like Banister's wife and sons, he too hates the killer more than anyone in this world. He wishes him punished and yet, when taking into account the circumstances surrounding the shooting, he can't really fault him either; perhaps if the man had been in the killer's shoes, he might have reacted likewise—struggling desperately to avoid complete humiliation, instinctively resisting anyone capable of exposing and ruining him. He'd pull the trigger, probably. By whatever means, he'd keep himself as unharmed as possible. He isn't above such violent impulses, he knows well enough: back in grade school, during a lunch recess, the man once struck his boyhood friend across the chin with a metal Jetson's lunchbox—knocking the boy down, silencing him; this after the boy had spotted Chad Teeger, a playground bully who disliked the man for no clear-cut reasons, and jokingly yelled: "Chad! Chad! He's over here—!"

Even so, he didn't kill or seriously hurt his friend—but, as he now accepts wholeheartedly, passive men can behave rashly in a threatening situation, real or imagined. While driving, while arguing, while attending sporting events—it happens every day. So, the man assumes, the killer is quite average, is married with children and holds a decent job, is generally respected by his co-workers and acquaintances— and if I were him, the man has often concluded when leaving the duck pond, I wouldn't lose any sleep thinking of my plight. Without a doubt, I wouldn't enter my mind at all.

And if sometimes the man pauses before going into the arroyo, standing stock-still at the edge of the park, it doesn't mean he is reluctant to return underground. On the contrary, he simply enjoys watching the sun's drift behind the distant mountains, at the same moment taking in his environment and the man-made flux which gradually, day by day, draws closer.

Real estate deals have pushed the suburbs further and further into the desert, bringing them toward the park and the arroyo and the tunnel. A mile or so east of the arroyo, where until recently only scrub brush and cacti thrived, a vast development of town houses and condominiums are under construction (cinder blocks, chicken wire, and brown plaster). But these new homes are not yet finished—and prior to the sun's fading, the man has envisioned them as being a cluster of the old adobe barrio homes which are still to be seen in various sections of the city.

Standing there—witnessing the onset of night, sensing the swift encroachment of mankind that both includes and excludes him—he has also pondered Tobias' words: "It's just dreams we're livin' in, buddy, I'm sure—right now, this here tunnel was just a dream in some other's head. Ain't our lives spent roamin' around someone else's ideas—everything we put on or in our bodies, the streets we call home, our homes, every little gadgety thing that makes us feel like we're unique and livin'? I'll tell you what—sure didn't have no say in the name I was given, didn't get no choices growing up that weren't already there for everybody else—did you?"

IN THE days and then weeks after Banister's murder, the man continued to function with little sleep, doing so methodically (napping just an hour or two following dinner), as if he were trudging upward toward the summit of a distant peak, proceeding because he must—gritting his teeth when smiling, replying vaguely when whatever question Julie had asked didn't fully register, pushing himself to keep busy all night inside the garage when his body ached from fatigue.

Suddenly one morning, as sunlight brightened the window behind his worktable, he turned around and saw that fall was arriving early. Outside, the serrated leaves on the mesquite tree had seemingly changed overnight, becoming yellowish and brittle; from his stool he observed some of the tiny leaves dropping, watched them flitter downward while recalling the afternoon he and Julie had planted the tree together (the day preceding David's first birthday, and the mesquite stood no higher than a yardstick).

Then, coming from the kitchen, he heard the momentary squeak of a faucet knob being twisted, the rush of water through pipes: Julie was already filling the coffee pot at the sink, her ritual before returning upstairs for a shower; soon she would rinse his coffee mug and set it on the counter beside her mug, a gesture perhaps symbolic of their union. Abruptly the man seethed, hitting the worktable with his palms. "How can you care for me?" he tried yelling, but managed an urgent whisper instead. "How can you love me?" The more he endeavored to shout, the quieter his voice became—"if you knew, if you knew everything, if you knew"—until, at last, the pipes hushed and only silence remained.

Later, while sipping coffee with Julie, he avoided looking her straight in the face; his eyes fixing on her mug, on her fingers wrapped about the handle, on the rim lifting past her breasts to reach her lips—and, smiling without understanding why, he nodded and spoke softly, saying, "Thank you, I needed this—it tastes great."

Afterwards, the man withdrew once again into the garage, feeling thoroughly expended and sluggish—like a zebra he had seen on the Discovery channel, the poor thing mired in a mud trap.

"Stuck—"

Sitting at the worktable, his head slumped forward, his eyelids pressed shut, and, as his breathing grew deeper, he grappled for a connection between that side of himself which had kneeled near Ronald Jerome Banister's corpse, and that other side which stood in broad daylight, enjoying television with his children or sharing coffee with his wife. But finding a connection proved difficult, especially when the zebra kept seizing his thoughts—how the creature struggled to free itself for hours, sinking deeper and deeper all the while, eventually slipping underneath.

"Got yourself stuck," he mumbled, drifting off. "You're stuck—"

Now, from the tunnel, the man gropes among his memories as he adds branches to the fire, as he promptly ignites the bark by blowing on the cinders. Gazing through the flames, he brings himself back home; he enters the garage and sees himself awakening at the worktable. He knows he will reach absently for his modeling glue before opening his eyes. Then, like a gambler considering the value of his poker chips, he will sort through his wood scraps, choosing the pieces he needs.

Yesterday he built a monoplane, today will be a stealth bomber—in four days he will create a Sopwith Camel, a compact, fairly rugged biplane used by the Allied forces. "In four days," he tells himself there, "you'll finish your last model and not even realize it."

Except his past self can't hear him, nor does this past self sense the impending upheaval: within forty-eight hours of completing the Sopwith Camel, Julie and David and Monica would exit the house for good, abandoning him as he sat alone and inarticulate at his worktable.

"I can't help you," the man tells himself. "Believe me, I wish I could."

Then he sighs, somberly shaking his head while forsaking his past self. Glancing away from the fire, he sees pure blackness beyond the tunnel's mouth.

Like being perched on the event horizon of a black hole, he thinks. Like existing at that place where whatever goes in might never come out again.

Still, the man is glad to be removed from that unsuspecting past self, though he very much misses the artistry of model building (sawing and then chiseling the fuselages, rounding the leading edges of the wings and tapering the rear edges, sometimes using a one-quarter inch dowel for the struts). The construction was usually simple, fairly rudimentary, requiring glue, wood scraps, often a wire coat hanger.

Yet the shaping of each model was, for him, a creative process which brought immense satisfaction—regardless of his distress regarding Banister's death, or the insomnia threatening his nervous system—and, as with the other models, the night he assembled the Sopwith Camel offered the same pleasure; except his satisfaction also harbored hope, a belief that everything—what he knew about the murder and his guilt for not coming forward—would get resolved the following morning.

Earlier in the evening, before shutting himself inside the garage, the man had already made his decision: after finishing the Sopwith Camel, after showering and dressing, he would drive downtown to meet Fred Rosas, the homicide detective leading the Banister investigation. Then, under the condition of anonymity, he would tell the detective what little he had heard at Mission Park—the brief scuffle, the gunshot, the motorcycle, Banister's final words.

When asked, the man would say he had simply gone there to use the toilet, nothing else (he hadn't seen anyone, he hadn't met anyone, but, frankly, he was aware of the restroom's infamous reputation; that fact, coupled with his job as a school teacher, he would shamefully explain, was why he didn't initially contact the authorities). Surely, he believed, the story would be truthful enough for Rosas.

And with his conscience finally cleared, the man suspected that Banister's judging eyes would forever close, allowing sleep to at last arrive with ease and without the possibility of nightmares; for how else could he begin the school year reinvigorated, his summer experiences filed into memory as a regrettable lesson learned? How else could he be the attentive father, the redeemed husband his loved ones deserved?

Nevertheless, in hindsight, the man wishes his decision to step forward had been based on something more meaningful than a late-night Crime Buster commercial. He now regrets that the hard choice hadn't stemmed from his children—a look of affirmation upon David's face before he kissed the boy goodnight, maybe Monica's little voice saying, "Love you too, Daddy"—or, at the very least, Julie snuggling against him in the living room, draping an arm about his shoulders while they watched *The Tonight Show*, waiting for the right moment to say: "Please don't take this wrong, okay? It's just that you don't seem yourself lately— you just seem out of it—and I wish you'd talk to me— because I can't help if I don't know what's wrong—so will you please tell me what's bothering you? You can tell me, you know that, right? You can tell me anything."

No, he thought, not anything.

Yet—from the accepting sound of her voice, the way she gently caressed his neck when speaking—he understood how badly she wanted him to reveal himself. But the best he could tender were the words she expected to hear, accompanied by a hand squeezing her knee, his fingers pressing into the pink fabric of her nightgown.

"Oh, everything's fine—just haven't slept well—guess I get antsy, you know, without teaching—I mean, you know what it's like being home and feeling like you should be working—makes me a bit anxious, I guess."

"Well, if you weren't eating I'd be seriously concerned," she said. "If someone isn't eating something's wrong."

He patted his belly.

He pinched a roll of fat, jiggling it underneath his shirt. "Nothing's wrong," he said. "Everything's good, honestly."

Apparently that was all Julie really required; his assurances were enough to ease her concerns, to bring her head against his arm as she gazed back toward the television and yawned. By the time the Crime Buster commercial ran, she had already trudged upstairs for the night, leaving him downstairs on the couch. Then, falling fast asleep, her snoring muted between pillows, she wouldn't witness her husband kneeling in front of the television screen, or glimpse his rapt expression as Detective Rosas and Angela Banister took turns addressing a video camera near the Mission Park toilet.

"On the evening of August fourth," said Angela Banister, "at approximately nine-thirty p.m., my husband Officer Ronald Banister was accosted inside the public restroom you see behind me—"

A brief re-enactment ensued, filmed in black and white and featuring her voice-over, depicting two male actors— one portraying Officer Banister, the other (heavyset, pony-

81

tail, leather jacket) acting out the assailant's role—both struggling violently in slow motion (a gunshot echoed, Banister collapsed, the assailant threw the weapon down and fled).

Detective Rosas appeared, rigidly facing the camera.

"I'm homicide detective Fred Rosas. A reward of fifteen thousand dollars is being offered for any information leading to the arrest and conviction of any person or persons involved in the murder of Officer Ronald Banister. Your confidentiality is guaranteed, all tips will be pursued."

The detective pointed a finger at the camera.

"So be a Crime Buster, let's take our city back!"

Throughout the entire commercial, Rosas' office phone number sat at the bottom of the screen, and, the second the announcement concluded, the man scrambled across the living room for a pen. Soon, when jotting the phone number on a Post-It, he sensed a lessening within his troubled mind, like an impossible equation had miraculously solved itself. *Confidentiality guaranteed*, he wrote directly beneath the number, underlining it twice.

"Confidentiality guaranteed," he said, suddenly feeling reprieved, somehow blessed.

And later, while building the Sopwith Camel, the man would pause, thanking the God he rarely ever acknowledged—thanks for letting Julie hold the remote, thanks for letting her pick Jay Leno instead of David Letterman ("You know, Letterman is so bitter these days," she had said, clicking through the channels. "Leno always looks like he's having fun."), otherwise the commercial might have been missed altogether.

Thank you, I've behaved recklessly—through your providence I'll change.

But during all the days since losing his family, he has lamented seeing Fred Rosas' face or the Crime Buster ad, and the God he now occasionally acknowledges receives only prayers of contempt—fuck you and your heaven, fuck the doom you've brought on me! Such a perverse God, he's positive, one who wasn't going to let the commercial go unseen, who wasn't content with the man walking out of the living room once Julie went upstairs—*if you'd spared me the commercial, if you'd just let me go grab a beer from the fridge and carry my guilt into the garage, I'd be a different person today.*

However, he can't deny that Rosas' guarantee of confidentiality gave him hope, made him breathe easier. And, regardless of what eventually transpired, God ultimately didn't keep him from grabbing a beer, or from going into the garage—though not before allowing him a final peek inside David's bedroom (how effortlessly the boy slept, snug between Pokemon sheets, bathed by the soft glow of an Elmo night-light).

Then he found Monica, the child having joined Julie in their bed (her ears seemingly oblivious to the snores growling past her mother's lips, her tiny chest touched by Julie's smooth palms).

Tomorrow, the man promised God that night, I'll put everything right, you'll see.

Tomorrow, he promised again while sitting at the work-table, a new leaf gets turned and I won't behave selfishly anymore or take my family for granted—I'm fortunate with a nice home, a job I value—and this wood gives me meaning, my hobbies give me my truest pleasure—I'm blessed—

The man rests his eyes in the tunnel, but resists sleep.

Previous moments, aimless and unforeseen, emerge like images flashed through a slide projector—David standing naked in the bathtub, the earnest students who crowded around his desk before class began and asked their questions, the alluring sight of Julie's once flat abdomen, Monica accidentally stepping on a hidden Easter egg, the emergency room doctor who stoically confirmed his father's death, the funeral procession soon thereafter.

Just then Tobias coughs from his sleeping bag, a short-lived hacking which punctuates the sonorous breathing; he shifts to one side, facing the tunnel wall, and resumes snoring.

Sitting beside the fire, the man opens his eyes; he glances toward Tobias, but instead fixes on the graffiti near the old guy's outstretched body: sprayed in black paint, faded over time, yet plainly visible even by firelight—GOD IS HERE. Suddenly he thinks he might cry, though no tears come.

Never before has the graffiti held any significance, so possibly—the man figures—an association was made when recalling his father's funeral procession; how, as a boy staring out of a car window, he observed a biplane's skywritten message, the words drifting over downtown Phoenix on that Sunday morning—HE IS RISEN. Somehow the slogan had given him peace, a small amount of needed strength; he could then stand graveside with his weeping mother, he could grip her hand, consoling her, and still steal glimpses of the distant skywriting, watching the message slowly evaporate into a clear blue sky.

Now the man imagines the Sopwith Camel's completion; its landing gear—coat hanger for the wire struts, length of one-fourth inch dowel for the axle, beer bottle caps for the two wheels—rolled across the worktable and then, rising upward between his fingers, the biplane began sailing overhead (for a while his fingers would become the pilot, his lips the droning engine). With an arm gyrating above the worktable, skywriting was performed, invisible messages fashioned to give him strength—YOU ARE RISEN, YOU ARE BELOVED, YOU ARE LUCKY.

Eventually, at dawn, the Sopwith Camel glided back to the spot where it had taken off, remaining grounded as the man left the garage and headed toward the downstairs bathroom (where he would strip, take a quick shower, brush his teeth afterwards). Subsequently, from the guest bedroom closet, he picked his most professional attire (blue button-up shirt, gray slacks, red tie, loafers, black socks).

Once dressed, he walked gingerly along the hallway, and stepped lightly down the stairs, slipping past the front door while Julie filled the coffee pot at the kitchen sink. Then, squinting against the morning sunlight, he strode forward with the Suburban's key poised in a hand (rush hour would soon find him waiting impatiently amidst traffic, absently humming along to an oldies radio station).

Within a block of the midtown police department, the man stopped at The Sunrise Cafe for coffee. One cup would lead to another, and another—until the caffeine had fully enlivened him.

He ordered an onion bagel and cream cheese, asked for a third refill of coffee. That was the hardest part, he recalls—finding the courage to leave the booth, pay the bill, and venture outside where the pay phone stood.

Then his hands trembled when he dialed Detective Rosas' number (too much caffeine, he convinced himself), and the pink three-story Spanish-style Police Department looming nearby heightened his agitation.

Just stay calm, he thought. Don't sound nervous, don't hang up.

In a matter of seconds Rosas was on the line, listening politely while the man hastily spoke.

"I'll try keeping this as brief as possible because I know you're probably busy except I have information regarding the Ronald Banister murder and I saw your commercial last night and so I figured it'd be a pretty good idea for me to get in touch with you—"

Obviously amused by the rapid-fire delivery, the detective couldn't have been less formal.

"Yes sir, I'd be glad to hear what you've got," Rosas said, his voice—a lively Hispanic lilt, somewhat mild and casual—almost settled the uneasiness inside the man's stomach. "You're also correct about me being busy at the moment—got someone on the other line—so you think you might come see me in person at, let's say, nine or nine-thirty?"

Only if Rosas would guarantee confidentiality, the man made clear.

Only if their meeting would be handled discreetly.

"You mentioned that on the commercial, that's what I want."

The detective didn't skip a beat, didn't hesitate in answering: "Sir, as long as you're not party to the crime, you've got my word—that's about the best I can give you."

"Okay," the man said. "Fair enough, I appreciate it."

"Last thing—got to get your name. Nothing major, just need to know who I'm expecting."

"Sure—"

The man paused, inhaling deeply.

"Sir, it'll stay between us, okay? I promise."

"Of course," the man said, "no problem—I'm John. I'm John Connor—"

Then moments later, after having reluctantly revealed his identity and after hanging up, the man spotted a pair of F-16s flying up beyond the city, soaring so perfectly in tandem, turning sharply west, then north, then east, finally zooming westward once again and disappearing over the desert.

A good omen, he believed that morning.

A very good sign, he had no doubt hours later.

But tonight, when returning to his sleeping bag, he imagines otherwise—not an omen or a good sign, not anything that meant anything.

Just forget it, he thinks now. Let it go and forget.

Then his entire body becomes warm, secure within the padding of the sleeping bag. Yet he is aware of the misgivings that won't leave him, always dogging his thoughts, and of the lingering vision of himself entering the downtown police department—and of the weariness which will soon subdue his mind. At last his eyelids droop and he begins drifting off (his limbs seem curiously buoyant as he rests there on his back, his exhales grow deeper and rhythmic, everything around him gradually fades into nothing). Both the past and the present recede, and, while Tobias continues snoring, the man is traveling beyond the tunnel; he is, for a time, floating somewhere far beyond his remembering.

II. Surface

ONCE INSIDE the downtown police department (after being directed upstairs to where Rosas expected him), John Connor quickly discerned that the reality of law enforcement was somewhat different than the gritty detective dramas or overwrought thrillers he had watched throughout his life, all those naturalistic crime shows depicting an abradable realness; contrasting such vivid stereotypes, the office space containing Rosas' cubicle was not a maze of cluttered desks with ringing telephones, of wary investigators bustling about a locker room-like environment.

Cigarette smoke didn't hang like fog at the ceiling.

Fluorescent tubes didn't flicker and hum overhead.

Instead, he entered a modern, well lit, seemingly proficient office corridor (gray industrial carpeting, standing partitions, computers and fax machines and Xerox copiers, not a hardened criminal apparent among the intent faces he glimpsed within the cubicles). No one, he observed, held a Styrofoam cup in a hand and sipped stoically while recording someone's statement.

A uniformed officer brushed past him, arms cradling a stack of thick manila folders.

"How's it going?"

"Good," he replied. "Yourself—?" he asked, but didn't look back.

"Pretty good," the officer answered from behind, the words trailing away as he spoke.

"That's good," he said, suspecting he wasn't heard.

No one was shouting, no one spoke too loudly.

Petty criminals weren't handcuffed to metal chairs and questioned.

Without a doubt, this wasn't a place where iconoclastic cops often erupted at their superiors during heated disagreements.

"Hello," a black woman said, glancing from her computer screen when he went by her cubicle.

"Hi," he said absently, continuing forward.

Like a corporation, he thought. Like a brokerage house. Cubicles on the right and on the left.

Ahead was a wall of full-length windows, which, as he approached, juxtaposed his reflection against a view of downtown buildings (his ethereal face and neck meshing with a parking garage, his eyes made gray from concrete). Then, realizing he was wandering aimlessly, he about-faced, returning to the black woman's cubicle.

"Pardon me," he said, "but I'm trying to find detective Rosas."

She looked up from the computer, her fingers still punching the keyboard.

"Just missed him," she said.

"I did?"

He checked his wristwatch.

"By about eight feet," said the black woman, grinning at either herself or the confusion evident on his face. Her hands left the keyboard and she pointed, indicating an adjacent cubicle. "He's next door."

"I see," he said, "must've walked right past."

"You sure did."

Overhearing their conversation, Rosas' voice suddenly came from the adjacent cubicle: "Mr. Connor?"

"Yes," he replied.

"Come on in," Rosas said. "Don't let Lea Anne scare you away."

He hesitated, staring at the black woman as she chuckled and pivoted her head back toward the computer screen. Then, resisting the urge to flee in the opposite direction, he found himself navigating those eight or so feet, stopping abruptly in front of Rosas' cubicle.

"There you are," Rosas said, reclining behind his desk, a newspaper spread limply across his thighs. "Have a seat." The detective waved him into a nearby chair; after that, while folding the newspaper shut and depositing it on the desktop, Rosas gazed at him inquisitively.

John shifted uncomfortably, crossing his legs, avoiding eye contact by scratching dirt off his left shoe. But whatever apprehension he had carried when stepping into the cubicle dissolved the second the detective said, "Want something to drink? We got Coke, maybe a fresh pot brewing."

"I'm fine, thank you."

"Water?"

"I'm all right, thanks."

"Let me know if you change your mind."

On the commercial, he remembered the detective towering above Angela Banister, appearing tall and robust, but in person he was actually smaller—wiry and lean, bespectacled, with a neatly trimmed mustache, thinning black hair—wearing a tan sports coat which seemed too big on him.

"So you saw me on TV last night."

"Yes. That's why I contacted you."

An immodest smile brightened the detective's face.

"Man, you've got no idea the amount of calls we've got just by putting my ugly mug on the screen—it's amazing. And now you're complicating my life by adding something else to the stacks—well, I'm all ears, my friend. Tell me exactly what you've got—"

John lowered his head, placing his hands in his lap. Then he paused, inhaling deeply before speaking. "Okay—," he said, glancing at Rosas, and proceeded to explain himself.

Ultimately, the meeting didn't take very long—probably less than forty-five minutes—but, in hindsight, he felt as if he had remained inside the cubicle for hours. However, the majority of his time was spent writing a statement, elaborating on everything he had already told the detective, adding minor details that weren't mentioned during their discussion.

"Make sure you get it all in there," Rosas said, handing him a pen. "Don't leave anything out, even if it doesn't seem pertinent."

Yet when talking to Rosas and then writing down the statement, he omitted any information he considered irrelevant or shameful (his real reasons for visiting the toilet weren't important, he reasoned; neither were Banister's final words—or the fact that he had disposed of his bloodied windbreaker). Only this mattered: he was sitting in a stall when the murder occurred; he heard the scuffle, the gunshot, followed shortly afterwards by what sounded like a motorcycle exiting the parking lot; he was terrified for his life, and, once he believed it was safe, ran from the restroom; the next morning he read about the murder, but, because the newspaper identified the toilet as a rendezvous spot for men, he didn't immediately inform the police.

Being a teacher, he concluded in his statement, *my initial concerns involved my job and how I would then be perceived by those I teach and those I work with. Regardless of my understandable need to use a public restroom, I became worried that my name would somehow get falsely associated with certain illegal behavior, as well as a murder, therefore blemishing my good standing, possibly resulting in damaging rumors which could harm me and my family.*

Needless to mention, I hope this confidential statement will correct my selfish reluctance, and, if nothing else, at least shed light on the tragic death of Ronald Banister.

At the bottom of the statement he signed his name.

Thereupon, Rosas asked him if had an e-mail address.

"I do, except I don't check it very often."

"That's okay. I'm just thinking that if I need to get in touch with you, I can do it by e-mail—that'll keep things private for you, okay?"

"Sure," he said.

Later, he would wonder if giving his e-mail address had been wise, especially since he checked his account at the school library. Nevertheless, he didn't worry too much, or fret over Rosas' erratic questioning, the way the detective had repeatedly interrupted him as he attempted to give a mostly truthful account.

"Let me stop you there. We have a report of someone in a leather jacket leaving the restroom sometime around the murder, was that you?"

"No, I don't own a leather jacket—I had on jeans, a blue windbreaker, sneakers—didn't see anyone in a leather jacket. As I said, I didn't see anyone at all."

"Right, of course, continue."

Then Rosas would do it again, breaking in while he cautiously related his version of that night, while he carefully weighed each particular before finishing a sentence.

"Sorry to interrupt—need the logistics—you stopped at Mission Park after going to which grocery store?"

"The Albertson's at Ajo and Mission, a bit far from where I live—but the Albertson's I usually go to was out of garden burgers—my wife eats those, she had a coupon—and I do our shopping—so sometimes I go to the other Albertson's—it's not that far from where I live, I guess."

Jotting a note on a legal pad, the detective would nod with understanding.

"I see, continue."

Except sometimes he wasn't allowed to continue. Sometimes his lips parted the moment another question sprang from Rosas.

"I'm sorry, but you say you're here now because you feel bad, somehow guilty about the murder?"

"Yes, the whole thing has wrecked me, made it impossible to sleep—had to get it off my chest, I'm exhausted."

"I can imagine—please, continue."

In the end, however, he was grateful for the detective's thoroughness, as it had kept him mindful of what words he chose. And when Rosas finally stood and shook his hand, he could tell the detective valued his assistance.

"Please know, I really do appreciate how difficult this was for you, honestly."

"Thank you," he said, his expression obviously one of relief.

Rosas gripped his elbow.

"You take care of yourself. Get some rest, okay?"

"Thank you," he said again.

Rosas patted his shoulder.

"Mr. Connor, it should be me thanking you," the detective told him. "Seriously, thank you for coming in."

The police department hovered in the Suburban's rearview mirror; then, like a mighty wind had shoved it aside, the building disappeared altogether. Driving from downtown, he cranked the radio volume, singing along with Bruce Springsteen as he passed rows of closely built barrio houses—some in grim disrepair, others freshly plastered—which gave way to a sloping concrete on-ramp.

Accelerating and converging amongst the highway traffic, he steered with his left hand—*in the day we sweat it out in the streets of a runaway American dream*—weaving around much slower cars—*sprung from cages out on Highway Nine*—while loosening his tie with his right hand—*chrome wheeled, fuel injected and steppin' out over the line.* At such a speed, he realized, even the smallest of sideswipes could produce a horrible aftermath.

How amazing, he thought, that society usually holds itself together—cars stay in their lanes, stoplights are obeyed, the rules are almost always followed. Rarely do people act so rashly, rarely does someone make an effort to plow into school children or deliberately drop their keys down a sewage drain. Yet throughout his adult life such troubling notions unsettled and entertained him—and, inexplicably, titillated him: he had imagined veering his vehicle into other cars or swerving toward oblivious pedestrians on the sidewalk, perhaps killing himself in the process. But, both hands now wrapped about the steering wheel, he sensed his own imperviousness, a remarkable ability to survive any ordeal unscathed. Then how promising and fresh everything looked outside (his fingers keeping beat, his voice chanting the song and creating new lines for lyrics he didn't know), how vibrant the world unexpectedly seemed.

The highway cut between a golf course and a shopping center.

On one side, golf carts roamed immaculate greens, and sand traps shimmered underneath the sun.

On the other side, cars traveled an expansive parking lot, coming to and going from Best Buy and OfficeMax and Wal-Mart; and beyond the shopping center, rising behind it, stood a four-level, dark-brown apartment complex.

As he sped further onward, similar apartment buildings appeared, standing at the fringes of suburban estates and beside small parks which punctuated the uniformity of development.

In every park, he observed, children played and teenagers shot hoops—so many little bodies, he thought, so many children—and at the park nearest his home a yellow kite flew above palm trees. The kite caught his eyes, floating effortlessly and alone in the clear sky.

Suddenly he began laughing, emitting a faint, inward chortle; he laughed when leaving the highway, when stopping for a red light. Then he laughed along neighborhood streets, all the way home and into the driveway, but stifled himself before climbing from the Suburban. Yet the strange delight reverberated, surfacing briefly as he contemplated the sunlight slanting across the front porch—seizing him once more after he found Julie in the kitchen, his presence startling her while she boiled hot dogs.

"My Lord, you scared me," she said, clasping a hand against her chest. "Could've given me a heart attack!"

Just then she noticed his clothing, and, without blinking, her expression went from distress to puzzlement.

"Thought you were sleeping—where've you been?"

He shrugged, moving closer.

At a faculty meeting was his explanation, getting ready for the fall semester.

And had he slept?

"Soon," he said, tugging on her shirt. "Very soon."

Soon he would remove his clothing in the guest bedroom. He would crawl beneath the sheets, vanishing until dusk—but first he'd kiss Julie by the stove, his affection confounding her.

"What's going on?"

"Nothing," he said.

"Go to bed."

She grinned, pushing him away.

"You're delirious."

"You wait," he warned, moving backwards from the kitchen, smiling slyly. "You just wait—"

Because after waking and showering and watering his plants, he planned on treating his family to dinner and a movie—two pepperoni pizzas delivered by Blackjack, *The Iron Giant* rented at Hollywood Video. Then he would sleep again (never once conjuring Banister's face, or jolted awake by fear), drifting off with a sublime contentment that, within just a few hours, would dissolve swiftly and permanently. Still, he would dream all the same, vast and intricate impressions that were mostly unretrievable upon waking.

Those oblique dreams—nebulous, so buried in his sleep as not to be fully recalled—couldn't hint at what had already transpired: that his windbreaker—specked with Banister's blood, containing a packet of lubricated condoms and an Albertson's purchase receipt—had recently been discovered by a sanitation worker; or that even while he sat inside Rosas' cubicle, other detectives were scrutinizing Albertson's surveillance videotapes—noting the exact time and date printed across the receipt—waiting to glimpse someone wearing a blue windbreaker, a likely suspect casually buying condoms approximately twenty minutes before the shooting.

Prior to stirring from his afternoon nap, the meeting had taken place in which the relevant section of videotape was examined by the entire investigative team; there Rosas spoke his name aloud, passing around copies of the written statement. Then, like fuzzy pixels finally forming an undeniable picture, the rest was fairly easy to surmise: on the night of August 4th, a schoolteacher purchased condoms at a grocery store; shortly thereafter he visited the public toilet at Mission Park. At some point he approached Ronald Banister by the urinals, soliciting the undercover officer. When Banister attempted an arrest, the teacher resisted and a struggle commenced. It wasn't known if Banister drew his gun, or if the teacher managed to remove it during the altercation. Regardless, the weapon was fired once, mortally wounding the officer, whereupon the teacher immediately fled from the scene. He disposed of his bloodstained windbreaker in an alley dumpster near Mission Park, a fortunate error of judgment (had the windbreaker been thrown away elsewhere, a mile further in any direction, it could have possibly escaped notice).

But what Rosas believed, what he had gathered from the written statement (disregarding for the moment John Connor's secret desire for sex with other men, or his violent opposition when fearing disclosure), was that the teacher harbored tremendous guilt for having committed such a horrible crime; his coming forward and offering information indicated this, the detective felt certain: in Rosas' mind, the teacher was an average individual, a novice criminal, who panicked and, considering the depth of his wrong, tried to absolve his conscience without implicating himself.

Yet several unanswered questions remained, and while the videotape footage and windbreaker seemed damaging enough, a little more evidence was surely required. So as he slept that afternoon, as he remained still and peaceful in the guest bedroom, a request for a search warrant was presented—once obtained, Rosas knew, the hard questions could start getting asked, the real inquiry could, at last, begin.

THE DOORBELL rang during *Good Morning America.*

And while Julie rose from the couch in her housecoat, her husband dreamt of a Japanese monastery, where an elderly priest swept the walkway cobblestones, whistling as five or six gray tabby cats emerged from underneath his robe; soon the cats would be climbing on him, purring and clawing his pants.

"Get them off!" he told the priest. "I'm allergic!"

The priest continued sweeping and whistling, paying him no mind.

By the time Julie unlocked the front door, finding detective Rosas waiting on the porch with his team of investigators, he would suddenly be elsewhere—gingerly traversing a steep hillside, pushing through dense foliage.

"Can I help you?" Julie asked, one hand attempting to straighten her disheveled morning hair, the other holding a cup of coffee.

"Sorry to disturb you this early," Rosas said, proffering a folded piece of paper.

"What is it—?"

Then how bewildered her slept-on face became as she absently took the paper, her eyes remaining fixed on Rosas.

"What's going on?"

"A search warrant has been issued for the premises—so I'd really appreciate it if you and anyone else here would please wait outside. Are you alone?"

"No."

"You're not alone?"

"No."

"Who else is here?"

"My husband, my son and daughter—that's all."

"No one else?"

"No, I don't understand—"

"I'm sorry," Rosas said, appearing remotely sympathetic. "You'll need to get your family together and wait outside, please."

The detective motioned for his team to follow, and, stepping past Julie, walked inside the house.

Now John was bathed in sepia—or, rather, it was the sky and the terrain, the cacti and the succulents around him, everything but his body made brown; his arms, outstretched as he strode onward, radiated with paleness; his pointing fingers, directing him across desert and toward a haphazard fortress built from red rock, looked like slivers of white bone unearthed amongst dry loam: somewhere a crow cawed, releasing a tormented cry which disoriented him.

"Get up."

Just then a harsh wind nudged against his back, and the crow called out once more.

"Did you hear me?"

Julie shook him awake in the guest bedroom.

"Get up, the police are here searching the house. Come on, they want us all downstairs. I'll be outside with the kids—get up, okay?"

She sounded abstracted, slightly robotic—and, opening his eyes, he wondered if he had heard her correctly.

"Julie," he said, turning over in the sheets.

Or maybe she had said something else altogether, something which was misunderstood within that place between waking and dreaming.

"Julie," he said again, sitting upright, watching her drift from the room, seeing her recede along the hallway.

Yet, for a while, his awareness remained hazy, unconnected (fragments of his dream briefly lingered—brownish clouds, brownish dirt). He floundered before climbing from the bed and leaving the room, slackly tying his robe when entering the hallway, combing fingers through his hair when wandering downstairs. Then, as if the vague recollections of his dreams gave way to a more vivid nightmare, he stopped, dumbfounded, at the bottom of the stairs, standing stock-still like an apparition lost amongst the living: men and women in dark blue T-shirts and black pants were everywhere, officious people methodically doing their jobs with white gloves on—some rifling dining room drawers, others lifting cushions or reaching underneath the couch, a few making notes on legal pads.

"Morning," said one of the men, brushing by him to jog upstairs.

"Morning," he mumbled, lowering his head and at the same moment thinking: *You promised me—we had a deal.*

A hand patted his shoulder from behind: "Listen, you'll need to stay outside, all right?"

He turned, discovering Rosas there beside him. The detective smiled, lightly squeezing his shoulder; then the gloved hand lifted, pointing an index finger toward the open front door.

"Don't think we'll be too long, Mr. Connor, but you'll have to wait outside with your family."

"Yes, of course," he said.

"We appreciate it," Rosas said, moving away.

Presently he went forward, absently touching the spot where the detective's hand had patted, going to where Julie stood forlorn on the porch—her arms folded, her miserable gaze seeking some explanation from him. He refused her stare, looking instead out into the yard: the morning light falling across the grass, so warm and inviting; the sunlight reflecting off the side mirrors of two police vans, off the chrome of four unmarked cruisers.

"Why are they here?" asked Julie.

"Don't know," he replied.

Still in their pajamas, David and Monica sat half-awake at one end of the front steps, quietly watching the investigators come and go empty-handed through the doorway (their hair occasionally ruffled kindly by those white gloves).

"What do they want?"

"Don't know."

His dazed expression didn't suggest betrayal or impending ruin, only confusion: Why is this happening? he wanted to ask Rosas. Why do this to me? We had a deal, you promised.

"I just don't understand," Julia said, and began crying, sobbing noiselessly, dabbing her tears with the collar of her housecoat. "I don't get it—"

"I don't either," he said, becoming conscious of several busybody neighbors loitering on the sidewalk, of cars slowing while driving past the house.

Anger suddenly revived him. He imagined finding Rosas, confronting the detective, and asking if so many vehicles were needed. Did they have to crowd the driveway, squashing the morning paper underneath a wheel? Because whatever they were looking for they wouldn't find. He hadn't done anything, he'd explained that already, *you sonofabitch*! They were messing with his life, creating a useless amount of trouble—*we had a deal, you fuck*!

In the end, however, it would be Rosas finding him, summoning him into the kitchen for a private talk. But by that point, after observing his toolbox carted from the house, all his indignation had swiftly eroded—and with his robe undone, he slouched before Rosas like a zombie, numbed, unable to meet the detective's eyes. Then what he heard seemed utterly ridiculous, a bit scripted: don't leave town, don't go anywhere, stay put.

"It's important you follow what I'm telling you."

Except he didn't follow; he was completely baffled: "Where would I go? I haven't done anything."

"That's good," Rosas said. "Everything's clear between us then."

"No, you can't do this like this," he whispered. "You're wrong doing this this way, you promised me."

He glanced up, glaring at the detective's face.

"Confidentiality guaranteed, you promised—"

Abruptly, as if a new investigator had taken over the case, Rosas' expression transformed. Gone without warning was the affable, grateful detective who, just yesterday, had been like an ally; in his place materialized someone harder, someone stern and extreme.

"We had a deal, you promised—"

Rosas leaned close, tying the belt on John's robe, tightening it while speaking lowly: "Let's get it straight, shall we? There's the ones that aren't really that queer—those that'll just fuck around I suppose with anyone for the thrill and excitement of doing it—then there's the pathetic closet cases—the ones that suck dick and get fucked—so what I want to know is—what I keep wondering about—which kind are you exactly, Mr. Connor?"

Taken aback, he couldn't respond, and, because the detective promptly turned and left the kitchen, perhaps the answer was already known. Subsequently, Rosas gathered the entire team, ushering them outside, shutting the front door behind himself. And even though the house had survived the search pretty much intact (the investigators having rifled considerately), and his children now proudly wore Crime Buster stickers upon their pajama tops (both ran into the kitchen to show him), and Julie had moved calmly toward the sink (rinsing her coffee cup, saying nothing), he felt unsteady on his feet, as if the ground had begun evaporating beneath him.

Sometime afterwards, he decided it was his desire to forget which made recalling that awful day so difficult. All the same, specific moments resonated acutely—such as

Julie coming into the garage, approaching his worktable: "Please say something, will you please—"

He sat there uncommunicative, hunched over in his robe. His hands fidgeted with scrap wood, organizing the pieces without purpose. He couldn't look at her, didn't have the wherewithal to acknowledge her presence.

"Please—"

Twice she came, hoping he might talk, keeping her composure even while delivering unwelcome news.

"There's someone on the porch—he won't stop ringing the bell. I'm worried it's a reporter."

Twice she came, and twice her temper inevitably erupted when he wouldn't speak: "Dammit, you tell me—why'd they take your toolbox? What's in it? What'd you do? I have a right, tell me why this is going on!"

He shook his head, parting his lips, but wouldn't speak.

Poor Julie, he thought, I'm sorry, I'm more upset than you are, believe me—please help me, please don't hate me, I'm sorry, I need you.

Twice she came, desiring a truthful explanation; twice she slammed the door shut on him.

"Damn you!"

Both times he silently cursed his inability to be honest with her—because, he concluded much later, she might have remained at his side, possibly as an outspoken advocate of his innocence; she could have forgiven him completely, he figured, had he confessed everything aloud and proclaimed his love for her. Yet it all crumbled so readily, making him believe that the years of marriage and family and home accounted for little when thoroughly tested.

Ultimately, he would try exiling that day somewhere beyond memory, attempting to forget how nerveless he was, incapable of exiting the garage or facing his children—how feeble and loathsome, not setting foot inside as late afternoon became night, terrified of what awaited him there

(Rosas and his team, a message from his school, the ringing of the doorbell).

So it was better to forget the anguish of his hours at the worktable—things he didn't do or words he should have uttered, mistakes made effortlessly. Moreover, there was comfort found when reflecting on the positive, recalling a single moment of peace which punctuated all that blackness: David sneaking into the garage just prior to his bedtime, bringing himself to the worktable, where he stood beside John in his pajamas, his small fingers gripping his father's arm.

"I'm going to bed now."

Only then could he speak, bending and hugging David tightly, saying, "I love you more than you know, you mean everything in the world to me."

He cupped his son's face in his hands. The boy's pupils were clear, lacking streaks of red, tinted with the china blue of a baby's eyes.

"God, I love you."

Devoid of emotion, David's eyes blinked at him.

"I love you too."

And before Julie could call for him, before David went running from the garage, he presented his son with the Sopwith Camel, explaining that, while more simplified than the jets and monoplanes they had built together, it was fashioned from good solid wood, and didn't need any painting on account of its attractive straight-grained appearance.

"Won't fall apart on you," he told David, allowing a smile as the boy zoomed the model through the air.

Bu-zzzzzzzzzzzzzzzz! Bu-zzzzzzzzzzzzzzz—

"Built to last," he said, watching as David flew the plane across the garage, his lips buzzing steadily like an engine, his body sailing full throttle toward his mother's weary voice.

BY THE time the sun brightened neighborhood rooftops, Julie had left with the children. First, however, she brought the morning paper into the kitchen, where she then sat on the linoleum and silently wept. Thereafter, she wrote John a letter, stopping every so often to brush tears from her face.

Finally she went upstairs, waking David and Monica. While helping both children dress and pack, she repeatedly insisted they remain as quiet as possible: "Whoever can whisper the longest gets breakfast at McDonalds, how's that?"

"Is it a game?"

"Yes."

"What if it's a tie?"

"If it's a tie everyone gets breakfast at McDonalds."

"Daddy too?"

"I don't know."

But John didn't hear his family go, all three vacating the house shortly before dawn. He never heard the jangle of Julie's car keys or David yawning when the boy stepped outside or Monica asking, "Where's Daddy?" Inside the garage, head lowered to the worktable, he didn't catch any hint of their swift departure—suitcases bumping down steps, the front door shutting and locking, the Suburban backing stealthily toward the street in neutral—nor, after sunup, did he sense what was missing (the water running through the pipes, the smell of coffee brewing, the habitual sounds of Julie beginning her day).

Though later on, as sunlight began sliding over the concrete floor, the unbroken stillness eventually insinuated their absence. Lifting his head, he realized the children's voices were gone—there had been no loud chatter at the dining room table, no sibling disputes abruptly shushed by Julie, no shouting or shrill laughter erupting somewhere within the house.

His limbs moved of their own accord, slowly and gingerly, taking him reluctantly from the worktable, impelling him into places he had wished to avoid.

"Please be here," he said, as if his words could make it so. "Please—"

He stared through a garage-door window, looking at the driveway, and saw only their old Mazda parked in its usual spot (that oil-dripping heap which had rarely been used since the Suburban's purchase).

"Please—"

His body pivoted, propelling him onward—out of the garage, through the laundry room, into the house.

His feet pounded across linoleum, his eyes searching around as he went.

Running upstairs, he tripped more than once on the steps while bracing a hand against the wall. Staggering wildly along the hallway, he at last called for them: "Julie—? Kids—?"

Each bedroom he entered suggested abandonment— David's unmade bed, Monica's empty top dresser drawer, the lamp glowing on Julie's bedside table even as the morning shone beyond the curtains. Then upon their mattress, which was perfumed with Julie's body lotion and retained the slight indentation of her form, he waited and shut his eyes while breathing into her pillow. The seconds between his inhales and exhales seemed, to him, like an eternity; yet every prolonged breath brought momentary hopefulness, a heartening feeling that Julie might be on her way home.

You'll return now, he thought. You'll find me here and come to me—you'll lie with me and hold me. You'll help me resolve these problems, and this unpleasantness testing your love for me will vanish completely.

Except she didn't return.

Presently, his fleeting hope became tainted by contempt. He found himself resenting her (she had somehow betrayed him), yet he refused to blame her (she had the right to betray him).

She would return, of course—no, she wouldn't return.

His mind alternated positions at an amazing speed; the contempt dissolved into self-loathing, the self-loathing bubbled into contempt again, like little David sharing his toys with Monica several years earlier: the boy tried his best to be generous, smiling earnestly while offering his toddler sister a stuffed brontosaurus doll. When Monica reached for it, David flashed an expression of outrage and smashed the doll against her chin. John too harbored such contrary feelings; he empathized with Julie wanting to leave him, but he also despised her resolve.

So on that glaring, warm morning, he climbed from the bed and wandered out into the hallway, shrugging off his robe as he advanced. Oblivious to his stomach's grumbling, he paused half-naked before the stairs, uncertain of what he should do next or how exactly he should proceed.

Maybe he trudged down the stairs without much effort.

Or perhaps he stayed for a while upstairs, peering at the steps below like someone perched upon a formidable precipice.

Not dissimilar to the fragmented scenes which predominated his dreaming inside the tunnel, he would recollect only ephemeral impressions of the minutes, possibly hours, afterwards—where, once bringing himself downstairs, he drifted about the house in a stupor, as if floating transparently through one room to another, his body scarcely disrupting the fine dust motes that glowed amongst sun rays.

Still, he would vividly remember the folded note on the dining table, a newspaper section beneath it and spread open, he imagined, for him to apprehend. But, frightened of whatever might be written in the letter or revealed in the newspaper, he didn't read either. Instead he turned away, ultimately avoiding the dining room altogether when walking and walking, pacing back and forth.

He wouldn't forget the answering machine in the living room, its red light blinking repeatedly. Eight blinks, he counted. Eight messages deleted intentionally.

"Stop it—!"

Or had he pushed the wrong button when trying to play them?

"Leave me alone—!"

Or had he already heard each message as he roamed the house, vaguely aware of who was calling?

"Just leave me the fuck alone—!"

His school's superintendent, Rosas, a hang-up, another hang-up, Rosas, a hang-up, Rosas, someone else he didn't recognize—though never Julie, no, never her voice summoning him, saying, "Are you there? Are you all right? Pick up the phone, please. Are you there? We're coming home, okay? Don't go anywhere—I love you."

Nor would he forget contemplating his own death, the idea of hanging himself inside the garage after setting the house on fire (a towline encircling his neck, tightening as he stepped off his worktable). And if he had been guilty—if he had been the person Rosas probably suspected him of being—John was positive he'd have fixed the noose weeks ago. But he wasn't guilty—at least not guilty of killing Banister. His crimes, he reasoned throughout the morning, were slight when compared with murder. Moreover, he had attempted to do right, and Julie needed to understand that.

"Don't punish me like this," he told her, appealing to their wedding picture on the living room wall. "Don't hate me—"

For a long, long time his fingers touched the glass of the picture. His palm pressed flat on Julie. Wearing a white bridal dress, holding a bouquet, she was staring at him from the past and grinning between his parted fingers.

"Forgive me," he said.

They had taken the picture in her parents' backyard, posing happily together during the reception. Now he envisioned her crossing the same backyard, her hands held by David and Monica. The three strolled amidst green hedges, luxuriating underneath the shade of palm trees.

You're far from this corrupt house, he thought. You've traveled to your real home.

Sometimes he would recall himself there, clutching the telephone while searching his memory for her parents' unlisted number. But, along with the children, Julie had taken that information. She had taken a lot more as well, countless small things he would have considered vital had he not gone underground—certain recipes he loved, the location of spare keys, the ability to pre-set the VCR timer, a general tidiness about everything she endeavored, her patience and gentleness.

The sun had crept above the living room windows, but a final shaft cut inside through a corner pane. It landed fully on his pale face by the phone, blinding him as he dialed randomly, pushing numbers with a thumb and desperately hoping, by some miracle, to reach Julie. Cupping a hand over the mouth-piece, he closed his eyes, put the receiver against an ear, and listened intently.

An operator appeared on the line: "What number are you dialing?"

He removed his hand, speaking urgently.

"I need assistance."

"Yes," the operator said, "how can I help you?"

He felt the shaft of light diminishing, its heat sliding from his face like a mask lifting. Opening his eyes, he gazed across the living room, focusing his attention on two objects he had seen all morning without grasping, until then, the indirect significance of them: the Sopwith Camel on the couch, a box of Monica's most valued Pokemon cards beside it.

"Sir, what number are you dialing? How can I help you?"

"You can't," he said calmly, and hung up the phone.

You'll return, he thought. You have no choice.

Indeed, he was surrounded by items essential to him and Julie and the children. Furniture. Clothing. Photographs. Toys. Videos. Scrapbooks. Those prized mementos, those treasured things—the proof and meaning of their existence.

You'll return.

For their sake he had to pull himself together. He had to stay in control, keep cool, otherwise they might leave again.

One thing at a time, he knew. Just relax.

Sensing the onset of fatigue, he rubbed at his eyelids, and, almost silently, whispered his father's mantra—the old guy's words soothing him as a boy, settling his troubled mind: "Formulate a game plan, figure a strategy, and don't worry."

He might have failed a final exam.

He might have performed poorly during baseball practice.

He might have accidentally run over a neighbor's dog.

"Don't worry—"

He might be suspected of a murder he didn't commit.

"Don't sweat it, kid," his father always advised. "Go outside, get some fresh air. Clear your head. Formulate a game plan—"

So that's what he'd do. But not before a hot shower, and not before shaving. Then he could go—driving the Mazda while clearing his head, glancing occassionally into the rearview on such a blazing, radiant day.

*   *   *

He gripped the steering wheel, squeezing it with white knuckles.

For several miles a blue van had been tailgating him, often speeding dangerously toward the Mazda's bumper. However, it wasn't Rosas following him, unless the detective had donned an elaborate disguise—thick black hair, a beard and sunglasses, seemingly Native American. In fact, as far as he could tell, it wasn't any investigator he'd observed yesterday at the house. Even so, he expected the arrival of more vans, the vehicles boxing him in as sirens erupted. When the van exited the highway, veering suddenly to the frontage road, his grip loosened on the steering wheel. Briefly, he searched the rearview, looking for similar vans or unmarked squad cars—though nothing imminent caught his eye, just the usual mix of lunchtime traffic.

Soon he too would exit, accelerating down an off-ramp and, seconds later, pulling into the parking lot of Del Rey Mall. Except it wasn't anxiety that finally sent him inside the air-conditioned mall, where he then strolled among teenagers and married couples and power-walking geriatrics; rather it was the relentless sunlight (so glaring and potent, somehow siphoning what limited energy he had left), urging him from the highway, from the confining Mazda, and past the sliding mall doors. For there he could become anonymous alongside strangers, a nonentity minding his own business—idly window-shopping, or wandering the isles of Amazing Discoveries (his hands touching toys and games he imagined his children would enjoy).

Yet—regardless of how invisible he initially felt—he remained hesitant and watchful, cognizant of those who approached and ambled by.

Was it likely, he wondered, that the weariness and fear showed on his face? Was it obvious to the people there that he wasn't anything like them, that if the sun could shine within the mall he'd be exposed as an impostor?

It was impossible to think straight, to clear his mind. As he had done at the house, he now paced the wide avenues of the mall, maintaining a circular course, each step seeming more difficult than the last. For a while he sat exhausted beside a water fountain, his head gradually slumping forward; then he revived again, gasping faintly, and rose unsteadily.

"Are you okay?" a teenager asked from behind.

He avoided turning.

"I'm fine," he said, quickening his pace.

"He's wasted," another teenager said.

Near the food court, a middle-aged Hispanic woman stared at him as he passed, her gaze hard and penetrating. Without glancing back, he knew her eyes were still trailing him, perhaps noting which direction he was going in.

What is it? he thought. What do you know about me?

On a bench situated between Radio Shack and The Gap, an elderly couple read sections of the daily newspaper, both glancing up when he drew close—their stoic expressions replaced with puzzlement as he walked by.

What have you read? What do you think you know?

He stumbled away, pushing forward with the realization that the mall was a grave error of judgment (to be truly nameless was to be completely unknown).

Who else was staring? Where were the other surreptitious glances, the whispers, the fingers pointing at his back?

Past the Sound Exchange.

Past Distinct Expressions.

Past the Sears where he and Julie once bought a humidifier.

"Julie—"

How badly he wanted to go home, to return and find her waiting with the children. Then, his head swimming, he cursed himself for not opening her letter, for being so afraid of what ultimately could have given him hope. She was his wife, after all, and loved him. She'd told him that two days earlier, kissing him before saying, "I love you." Furthermore, it was something she would surely mention in the letter, like she had in previous notes: *Love ya, Julie.*

Real love, he believed, didn't die overnight. Their love, the affections professed over years, had nothing to do with newspapers or the curious stares of strangers—or Ronald Jerome Banister.

He panicked and spun around; startled by the various people roving about him, he fled.

For a moment every face considered him, every pair of eyes shot his way, and he zigzagged through crowds which appeared like blurs.

Careful, he was told.

Watch it, someone else yelled.

He didn't slow until reaching the parking lot, until climbing safely into the Mazda—where he sat motionless while catching his breath, so as not to black out.

Afterwards, when driving home, he stayed conscious by muttering the lines he had prepared for Julie. He'd say, matter-of-factly, that his recent behavior and lack of communication were inexcusable. He'd then explain everything—the sleeplessness, the arcade, the Mission Park toilet, the murder, how Rosas had complicated the situation horribly ("The detective betrayed my confidence—he's barking up the wrong tree, believe me"). He'd be straightforward, underlining his remorse, his shame, and—with her supporting him—his ability to change. Like Paul, the apostle to Nations, he had seen the light, his unsettling baptism occurring the night Banister was killed (Julie would understand that; she would, however upset, offer her forgiveness).

Though what he planned on saying inevitably went unheard, and whatever Julie had written would forever remain unknown: for he hadn't expected the three squad cars parked in front of their house, the one or two neighbors loitering nearby. Surely Rosas was there too, somewhere inside (opening closets, looking underneath beds, exploring the garage, speaking his name).

His face expressed nothing, even as he uttered, "Fucker—!"

The Mazda slowed, allowing him just enough time to peer at the driveway to confirm that the Suburban was still elsewhere: You can return, Julie, but I can't now.

"Bastard—!"

Then, before continuing, he noticed his neighbor Jacob—that retired accountant he had rarely addressed, that apparently shy fellow with a wife dying of breast cancer—standing beside his mailbox, holding a rake, gazing blankly at the Mazda. To John's amazement, Jacob didn't move, didn't promptly rush next door and inform the police—he didn't do anything except stare.

All of a sudden numb, he drove on (at that very moment, he concluded weeks later, a dense fog obscured the familiar, leaving him lost in the world). He steered without thought, traveling aimlessly—avoiding the highway, cruising residential streets, escaping into the heart of downtown. Frequently his eyelids sagged, his head bowed and jerked upright. Yet he managed to stay on the road, to brake for stop signs and red lights. The downtown thoroughfares were busy, the sidewalks bustling; in a few hours those thoroughfares and sidewalks would be about as lively as he felt. So again he made circles, back and forth upon the same succinct route—past the main library, the barrio mission, the Amtrak station, the main library—

The brown-stucco buildings bled together, numbing his mind and his eyes, until evening approached and he found himself taking refuge behind the Amtrak station, parking several yards from the tracks. Already the station was deserted, but, with the gas meter registering on empty, he didn't care. He had nowhere to go, and he was beyond exhaustion. As always he would wait, becoming more accustomed to the gradual compass of hours, like the repetitive patterns on wallpaper—the design of his fruitless, continual languishing. Soon he'd embrace that kind of protracted idleness. He'd wrestle doubt, hoping for affirmation, redemption, denial of denial, the mastery of indecisive biding.

But now he would rest, reclining his seat as dusk loomed. In the seconds preceding sleep, he formulated his shoddy game plan, figured his uncomplicated strategy: in the morning he'd purchase a train ticket with a Visa card, stepping onboard while Rosas was probably searching highways and hotels for an oil-dripping Mazda. Of course, his credit card would get traced, but he figured he could disappear beforehand (lying low in some dusty little town, or at least finding a way to locate Julie and the children).

He couldn't devise any more than that—at once his body slackened, his head slumped. How quickly sleep took him, washing over him like swift death, and shielded him, for a while, from the blaring of train horns, the earth's vibrating, the immense comings and goings sweeping before his windshield.

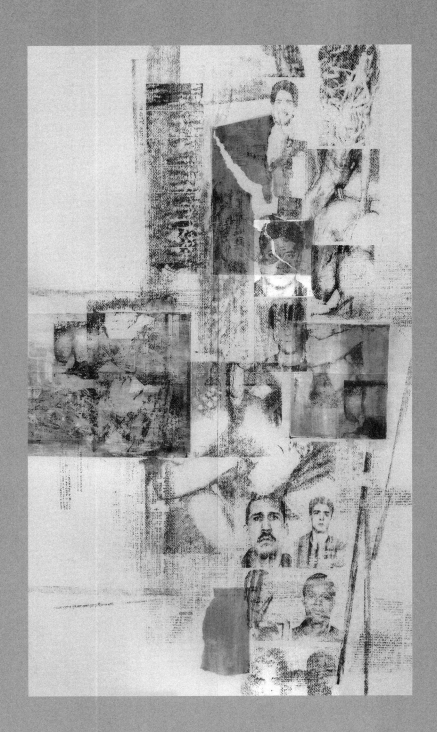

SHARING A dining car table, he stared through the window beside him, watching as a full moon followed the train and the city slid past outside—warehouses, barrio homes, headlights moving along the highways.

Soon only the moon remained, hanging brightly over flat, outstretching desert and winding arroyos (sometimes over isolated, silhouetted cabins or shacks left unoccupied, perhaps, near trestles and embankments).

On the other side of the table sat Polo, rigidly probing his dinner with a fork while refusing to eat: "It doesn't look done—this salmon doesn't look cooked."

He wouldn't face Polo, or acknowledge his presence—staying aloof even as Polo, every so often, patted him underneath the table in an affectionate, discreet manner. Polo wasn't ruffled by his companion's indifference, maintaining his calm when studying him circumspectly, eventually putting the fork aside and saying, "You know, you aren't alone—"

He awoke inside the Mazda, stirring into darkness, where the nebulous world he'd just emerged from was eclipsed by the squeal and grind of a freight train's wheels. Then it seemed as if he was observing himself in the seat, somehow seeing the cold perspiration across his forehead and neckline.

Adjusting the seat upright, he suspected he had slept until almost daybreak, but, when consulting the digital clock on the dashboard, he realized it had been less than five hours. Now midnight was approaching, and yet he felt thoroughly rested, as though a good many hours had transpired since he had parked the Mazda at the station.

The freight train rattled away, squealing further down the tracks; the ground settled in its wake, the Mazda ceased vibrating. At last gone, the train no longer obscured his view. Slowly exhaling, he glimpsed the stars, the downtown buildings, and the chain-link fence running parallel to the tracks. Inhaling deeply, savoring the silence that ensued, he breathed the muskiness rising off his collar—a faint scent recalling the aftermath of sex, of skin glazed with sweat— and the odor gave him a pleasant, relaxed feeling, a slight weariness, hinting at where sleep had taken him.

"You know," Polo had said, "you aren't alone."

Polo had squeezed his knee underneath the table.

"I know the truth. I know—"

The underlying meaning of Polo's words didn't immediately surface, though what was said continued to resonate—persisting as he climbed from the Mazda and locked the doors, as he stepped to the rear of the car and urinated on the ground.

You aren't alone.

Then, zipping his pants, it struck him: someone knew he was innocent, someone could prove he wasn't involved in Banister's death.

I know the truth.

If Rosas spoke with Polo, if Polo could just talk to Rosas—if Rosas would realize his mistake—then, he assumed, the current mess with Julie might get properly resolved.

I know—

However, like Banister's killer, the identity of Polo was another mystery. Moreover, he understood that revealing Polo to Rosas was to also confess his true reasons for visiting Mission Park (those reasons obviously already gathered by the detective, no doubt functioning as the springboard for any suspicions). Still, the reality of Polo

124

seemed important and somehow helpful, especially considering how everything was unexpectedly stacking up against him.

So, he reasoned, Rosas must know the truth. At the very least, the detective should hear a description of Polo, should listen and comprehend that someone else was there at the Mission Park toilet.

Stomach pangs suddenly tightened his gut. Breathing heavily, he stooped, hugging his chest until the pain subsided.

How long since eating? How long since anything passed his lips?

Yesterday? Or two days previous?

He couldn't be sure.

He reached into a pocket, feeling for change. Then, crossing toward the Amtrak building, he counted coins in the dark—six quarters, two dimes, a nickel, some pennies—surely enough for a candy bar, maybe two, and a phone call.

Once inside the mostly empty station—where a vagrant slept on a far bench and an elderly counterman thumbed through a magazine—he waited his turn at the vending machine, standing behind a Mexican woman and her small daughter. The woman was having trouble deciding what she wanted (a Grandma's Cookie, or a Twix, or—?); completely bewildered, she studied each snack methodically, an index finger pressed to the plastic window—and all he could do was glance around the station, which, bathed in fluorescent light, smelled vaguely of cigarette smoke and body odor.

"Go ahead," the woman said, moving aside. "Too many choices."

He nodded, saying nothing.

Without deliberation, he purchased cheese crackers and a Milky Way, devouring both while en route to the restroom, his stomach instantly satiated. Shortly thereafter, he stood at a sink scrutinizing his reflection in the mirror above it—the unkempt hair and black stubble dotting his chin, the bruise-like discoloration on his lower eyelids that recalled, to his mind, a raccoon.

Nearby, a heavyset Mexican gentleman (the husband of the woman, he figured, and the father of the girl) was busy brushing his teeth, pausing occasionally to run water over the toothbrush.

Avoiding eye contact, he wet his hands, splashed his face and neck.

He combed damp fingers through his hair.

He rinsed his mouth, gargling and spitting, gargling and spitting, chocolate and cracker residue swirling down the drain.

"Here," the gentleman said.

Glancing sideways, he saw that he was being offered toothpaste.

"Thank you."

He took the tube, putting a dot of Crest on a fingertip.

"Thank you," he said again, giving the toothpaste back. Then he brushed his teeth.

Moments later, while washing their hands, the gentleman asked, "You on your way to L.A.?"

"Yes," he said, and, feeling the inexplicable need to elaborate, added: "My sister lives there."

The gentleman dried his hands on his shirt, saying, "Me and my family are coming from El Paso." He turned, wandering toward the restroom door. "My parents are in L.A., so we're paying them a visit—if the damn train ever gets here."

"When is it due?"

The gentleman shrugged, pushing the door open.

"Soon, I hope. It's running an hour late."

Now alone in the restroom, he quickly dried his hands, wiping his palms along his pants legs, before checking the contents of his wallet. Forty-six dollars, not enough for a train ticket. But he had his credit cards, and, if Julie had paid the bills on time, he could create a diversion from

126

Rosas: "If I leave the city," he wished to tell the detective, "I have every right—I haven't killed anyone!"

So he would buy a ticket for Los Angeles; although prior to approaching the counterman, he huddled at the station pay phone, dialing Rosas' office number, ready to explain everything. Except he hadn't considered the hour, forgetting that the detective wasn't working yet. Instead he talked to voice mail, urgently whispering what needed to be said.

Yes, he had frequently gone to Mission Park for sex.

Yes, he was there for sex on the night Banister was shot.

Yes, he was ashamed to confess the truth, but it didn't matter anymore.

And he was innocent.

And someone could prove it—someone whose name he didn't know.

He mentioned Polo's description, how often they had met, the Dockers and the cologne. He said Polo was probably married, Polo heard the gunshot, Polo and he were together when Banister died.

"You've got it all wrong, and he'll put you straight—he knows I haven't done anything. Take what I'm saying seriously because you have an obligation to find him—that's all I have to say to you—that's it—"

Upon hanging up, he heard the train rumbling to a stop outside, its arrival a mixture of creaks and hisses and metal clanking. Immediately the Mexican family began gathering their belongings (the wife cradling her purse like it was a baby, the father hoisting a green suitcase with neon flower patterns, the daughter toting a plastic bag containing oranges), all three hurrying through the swinging doors and stepping onto the platform.

By then he was already at the ticket window, handing the counterman his Visa card: "I need a one-way to Los Angeles."

Shutting his magazine, the counterman eyed him haltingly for a second, and John worried that he might be recognized. The counterman abruptly yawned, consulting his watch, then said, "She just got in, but we can get you taken care of—you want a sleeper or coach?"

"It doesn't matter."

"Well, I'll tell you, a sleeper is more expensive."

"Coach is fine."

Afterwards, he loitered on the platform, standing by the family, watching as a smattering of passengers departed the train and wandered sluggishly toward the station—some pausing momentarily to breathe the night air, others trudging forward with suitcases and backpacks. The father reached for his daughter's hand, tugging her slender arm, gently pulling her behind his wife who was walking briskly ahead of them. Presently the three would go aboard, and soon, he knew, they'd fall fast asleep while that train sped westward.

But the journey he was about to begin wouldn't involve train service or take him very far—even though tracks would still be required: for once the train left without him, becoming a diminishing red light in the distance, he proceeded on foot—walking between rails, stumbling amongst darker environs, tearing his ticket into pieces and letting the bits flutter to the ground like snowflakes.

And, he imagined, by the time the authorities traced his Visa card—by the time they had searched the Mazda and boarded the train somewhere in California and directed questions at oblivious passengers—he'd be sitting beside the tracks, taking a break, and waiting for the sun to finally rise above the Catalina mountains.

How improbable, he considered later in the day, that life could change so abruptly—that one could suddenly lose his family, his home, and, within hours of such upheaval, find himself drifting down railroad tracks, sent into bar ditches when trains approached, sometimes startled by the barks of guard dogs when passing warehouse fences. But he wasn't drifting aimlessly, or without scope, and shortly after dawn his roaming brought him close to Mission Park—where he then ventured out into the desert, leaving the tracks, trekking toward the park which, visible a mile or so ahead, loomed like an oasis.

Soon he would enter the curving dirt paths and welcomed shade, moving beneath palm trees, walking around the outgrowth of mesquite branches. Before noon he'd nap under the cover of a dense hedge row, his body stretched between foliage and the red-brick wall enclosing the public swimming pool—his fitful rest disrupted by children yelling, the diving board's continual tremor, water erupting from cannonball jumps.

Nevertheless, the swimming pool noise didn't bother him much, nor did the racket of lawn mowers crisscrossing the park grounds. He enjoyed the steady commotion, the strange rhythm of human dissonance, while remaining aware of the fact that come evening the park would be a hushed place, the children's voices vanquished by a soft breeze, and the occasional lament of wildlife.

Then, unseen in darkness, he'd push through the hedge row, beginning what would eventually be his ritual: going cautiously into the night, hiking to a picnic table near the public toilet, spending hours there (concealed amidst mesquites, keeping as vigilant as possible, never turning from the public toilet, always noting the men who sauntered underneath the pathway lights); he'd wait patiently for Polo's return, praying his former companion would still come to bend in the back stall as a stranger's erection shoved inside him. Once Polo was spotted, he conceived of rushing to the pay phone, dialing a 911 operator, and saying, "I'm at Mission Park, please send someone quick—a witness to Roger Banister's murder is here!"

His plan was as simple as that.

Naturally, he assumed it was a long shot, reasoning that if Polo sought public sex he wasn't likely to do so where the murder had occurred, where he had been so thoroughly shaken (unless, of course, such an event might heighten the risk and eroticism of the Mission Park toilet). But he believed it was a chance worth taking, made all the more viable by those he spied during his first watchful night (the solitary men strolling in and out of the toilet, the cars now and then circling the parking lot). Apparently, Banister's killing had done little to quell the same illicit activity John too had partaken of; except his recent meetings at the toilet seemed like they belonged to another lifetime, and, while maintaining his vigil, he never saw anyone remotely resembling Polo, only middle-aged men and one overweight Hispanic teenager—each entering the toilet at various times throughout the night, exiting minutes thereafter and heading promptly to their vehicles.

Still, he did see at least one familiar face: a tall Indian fellow with wire-rimmed glasses, early thirties, who arrived at the toilet with his partner or friend (a stocky white guy, clean-cut, perhaps a couple of years younger). Both disappeared into the toilet together, but, less than a minute later, the Indian fellow came outside alone—pacing the sidewalk, smoking, evidently acting as a lookout. That's when he remembered him, though he wasn't sure if their encounter was at the toilet or the arcade. What he clearly remembered, however, was the fellow on his knees, masturbating him until sperm ejaculated across his chin and mouth. Now the fellow leaned casually against the pay phone, flicking ash as his partner lingered within the toilet.

Lovers, he concluded. No longer satisfied by what the other offered sexually, both always wanting someone new, something provocative. An arrangement of sorts, he envisioned, a middle ground—they keep one another and fuck whoever else and afterwards they'll sleep in their bed, arms and legs entwined, glad for the warmth given by a tangible body with a tangible identity.

Yet on that night, as on subsequent nights, he never once felt a kindered pull toward the toilet, to briefly slip past the entrance and—forgetting his troubles, escaping from the unfair world which existed beyond the doorway—unzip his fly for an open mouth, for someone's expectant tongue. Instead, at dawn, he found himself pitying those men while crawling into the hedge row.

Such fools, he thought, stretching along the swimming pool wall. You're stupid and selfish—and, like myself, you'll realize it too late.

Hunger pained his stomach, but he didn't care. Folding his hands upon his belly, he suspected he could survive days without food, perhaps weeks. A very small price to pay for proving one's innocence, he decided. A very small price.

It was often there—when verging on sleep behind the hedge row, or when waking to the sounds of children splashing into the pool—that he began weeping for Julie and David and Monica, speaking their names under his breath, hoping they'd ultimately come home and find themselves missing his presence: he'd beg their forgiveness, he'd make amends again and again, he'd rebuild their lives together.

"I promise—"

But first he had to find Polo—then he could rebuild.

"I promise," he'd say, lulled by his own voice. "I promise—"

FOR THREE nights he staked out the Mission Park toilet without eating, sipping only from a Gatorade bottle which he had found empty beside a trashcan, rinsing it clean in a drinking fountain near the swimming pool, filling it with water. If hunger raged, threatening the nightly surveillance, he drank until his stomach felt heavy—sometimes replenishing the bottle several times before setting off across the park. Then when urinating, he did so discreetly, usually at the same mesquite tree, and never once approached the toilet to relieve himself.

On the fourth evening—after waking with trembling hands, with barely enough vigor to crawl from the hedge and stand up—he realized food was needed; otherwise he might become too weak or disoriented to sustain his watch. So, as the sun began waning, he headed in the opposite direction of the toilet, going unsteadily and slowly from the park—past the entrance gate, over a small bridge, beside construction sites, along sidewalks.

Eventually he arrived at a foundering strip mall, where a few businesses continued operating amongst vacant storefronts, plywood sheets covering windows and doorways, lease signs made incomprehensible by spray-painted graffiti. Yet a Burger King thrived in the middle of the parking lot, the franchise teeming during the dinner hour. Located on the far northwest corner of the strip mall, Quan's Oriental Market was busy too, the parking spaces around it lined with vehicles, the bright interior glowing beyond its gaping warehouse entry. Everything else between the two—

aside from a pet shop and a tortilla factory—had been boarded shut.

But it was the aroma of Burger King that drew him closer (a charred, meaty scent fuming through rooftop vents, carried by the breeze), bringing him to stand outside the front window. Peering inside, he saw others eating—families and couples and kids and solitary souls, all lifting french fries or putting lips on straws, fingers grasping Whoppers or carrying trays; ordering at the counter or seated before their meals, no one paid attention to him, even as his legs faltered for a moment, his body sagged forward, and, fearing collapse, he braced a shoulder against the window.

Don't keel over, he thought. Not here—

He could see himself there, hovering inches from the glass, no longer gazing inside. His reflection blinked back at him, helplessly. He noticed the puffiness and circles underneath his eyes, the pallidness of his flesh, the facial hair which had grown thick upon his jawline, neck, and cheeks. Then to his surprise, he realized the past five days had disheveled more than just his mind: now he looked like a castaway, or like one of the vagrants he spotted prowling Mission Park—ruffled and gaunt, sockets sunk deep into the skull.

However, his haggard appearance wasn't wholly an unsettling sight; in a way, as he pushed gingerly from the window, summoning his remaining strength, he was glad for the transformation, sensing a degree of freedom to be had with the masking of a baby-faced school teacher, someone who once shaved most mornings and combed his thinning hair and dressed appropriately. Glimpsing that face, that receding reflection, he fathomed an entirely different person—and within two weeks, he imagined, the beard would be so thick and peppered, the hair so matted and oily, he might wander without regard, perhaps seeming no different than those weathered transients at the park.

Until then, he wouldn't risk entering the Burger King, regardless of how tempting the food was or how badly he required nourishment (his decision hastened by a young woman seated at a nearby booth, casually reading a newspaper while she ate).

So he promptly moved on, drifting gradually toward the oriental market—where, as if transported miraculously overseas, he would soon travel down its wide aisles holding a grocery basket, lingering before bins of bitter melons, bamboo shoots, and fresh bean curd.

For a while his hunger lessened, somehow calmed, he believed, by the strangers around him: men and women talking in Mandarin or Vietnamese at the seafood department, Asian students hoisting bags of long grain rice into carts, slanting-eyed children clutching Morinaga caramels while running up the aisles; none of them pausing to consider an ill-at-ease white man bagging apples and pears, an alien among aliens reaching for packets of dried squid shreds—a snack he had enjoyed during his school's Heritage Week, reluctantly sampling the jerky-like squid at a Japanese student's sincere urging.

How puzzling, he thought, to become invisible to those who are often invisible elsewhere—those like faces and eyes, those indistinct voices making the same unintelligible sounds.

"Dwae bu chi, ne mai bu mai da doe?"

He could be in Taipei, pacing the narrow avenues of the night market.

"Che ka duo shou chin?"

He could be strolling through a Beijing shopping district, breathing the exotic: spicy mole plant sprouts, bitter tea, storax gall, chrysanthemum, hot pickled soybean sauce.

"Che mo na mo kway ah?"

He could be thousands of miles from that southwestern Burger King—a tourist far from home, standing at a checkout counter in Hong Kong, telling the Chinese cashier,

"I'll take this too," when adding a daily newspaper to his purchase.

Leaving Quan's and crossing the parking lot, walking over asphalt illuminated by yellow lights and shuffling past the desolate storefronts, he returned to the familiar—heading for the park with a small sack of groceries, a newspaper sandwiched under an armpit, his fingers wrapped around an apple like it was a baseball. By the time he resumed his stakeout three apples had been consumed, the cores gnawed apart and then discarded. Now sitting on the picnic table, he bit into a pear (the dried squid shreds being saved as his final meal prior to sleeping) and monitored the toilet activity.

Except that night would be like previous nights—men came and went, some making repeat visits hours later, though Polo never arrived. Still, he waited, scrutinizing every figure that approached the toilets, every leisurely entrance and swift departure, wondering all the while: Did you kill Ronald Jerome Banister?

Was it you?

Or you?

Or you?

He looked for motorcycles.

He kept an eye out for undercover cops, for police squad cars cruising the park grounds.

He prayed the killer would strike again, shoot someone at another park, get caught afterwards, and confess his crimes to a guilt-ridden Rosas.

Sometimes he envisioned catching the killer himself, wrestling him to the ground, knocking him unconscious with his fists, finally dragging the wretch into Rosas' office and throwing him down before the shocked detective: "Here he is, you rotten fuck!"

Or Polo would show up, startled by John suddenly accosting him, but nevertheless pleased.

"You've got to help me!"

"Of course—"

"They think I murdered Banister."

"I know—"

"You'll tell them they're wrong. You've got to help."

"Of course—"

Ultimately, however, his fantasies of redemption always fell away, and he was left with nothing. Only then did he despair, doubting that Polo would ever set foot in Mission Park again. So he gave himself two weeks. Two weeks of waiting, fourteen days of watching the toilet—after that he'd widen his search, perhaps exploring other parks, or, if need be, observing the rest area toilets on the outskirts of the city.

I'll find you, he ruminated throughout the night. We'll meet again and I won't let you disappear. I'll find you—

At dawn his apples and pears were finished, the remnants scattered about the ground and set upon by ants. Sunrise had once again signaled an end to the toilet's nocturnal activity, and, as warblers began calling from palm trees and mesquites, the park was a peaceful place for a time, devoid of any human comings or goings. Relishing the morning on a full stomach, he shook the newspaper open, spreading it upon the picnic table. He scanned the front page—underlining headlines with an index finger, expecting his name to materialize—but found no mention of himself whatsoever.

He flipped the page.

Nothing.

The next page.

Nothing.

And just as relief crept into his mind, his finger slid across seven words at the top of 4A: BANISTER SUSPECT SOUGHT BY AUTHORITIES IN CALIFORNIA. Below the headline was his passport picture, a fuzzy black-and-white taken four years previous. Reading the article, discerning from the report that the investigation had been successfully diverted, a curious mix of dread and elation consumed him. He had, in effect, sent the detective and his team on a wild-goose chase, conceivably allowing himself more liberty to roam unrecognized.

Given enough time, he assumed, noteworthy dramas would render him obsolete. The next major tragedy—a murder, a rape, a drive-by shooting, the death of a child—would banish him from everyone's consciousness (everyone save the investigators, Banister's family, and his own). Whereas five days previous he was surely front page news, today he hid on page four—in a month he'd likely be nonexistent. So he'd grow the beard, test his freedom by degrees (a walk here, a meal there, a bus ride when his legs became too sore). And without question he'd encounter Polo again—even if it took weeks or months or years.

I'll find you—

Then later, using the newspaper as a pillow, he slept soundly within the hedge row, undisturbed by the swimming pool splashes, the shrieking of children. He'd awake come evening—and for the next twelve nights he was unwavering in his routine: going to Quan's Oriental Market, buying food and a newspaper, eating his meals while anticipating Polo, climbing into the hedge row at dawn.

I'll find you—

But after twelve nights, two days shy of his two-week goal, he decided at last to leave Mission Park and search elsewhere; his choice was determined less by Polo's absence than it was by the young man who had invaded the hedge row: "Listen, I'm Barton, all right? And I don't care what you call yourself, as long as you fuck off!"

Barton—no first name, no last name—just Barton.

"Like Sting," the kid contemptuously told him. "Like Madonna."

He hated the very sight of the boy—those dreadlocks and thick sideburns, the pimply complexion, the green camouflage pants, the black Bob Marley T-shirt, that tattered cashmere overcoat.

"Barton, that's me. One word, got it? Barton."

Like Cher.

A poor excuse for a living thing, he thought. A filthy, self-serving punk—recently found sleeping in the hedge row, stretched out where John had always slept. Furthermore, Barton had claimed the newspaper stash as his own, creating a makeshift mattress from it. Still, he tried reasoning with the kid, explaining politely that the hedge row was his domain, the newspapers were all his, the apples Barton had helped himself to were also his.

"Hey, you don't own the park, okay? And you don't own me, all right? So you can fuck off before I waste you. Anyways, I've slept here plenty and you weren't nowhere around—so I'd say I've got more rights here than you do, got it?"

Like Attila, the scourge of God.

"But you ate my apples, Barton."

"Fuck your apples, and fuck you! You eat my shit if you want your apples!"

Like *profane.*

"I think you're being unreasonable."

"Oh fuck you!"

Like *affliction.*

The last straw came the next morning when he entered the hedge and discovered Barton having sex—the kid half-naked and groaning lowly, thrusting between the splayed legs of a woman twice his age; his pale ass flexed rhythmically, the newspapers crumpling underneath the woman as she arched her spine (John had seen her on occasion, digging through trashcans, her skin like leather and her hair unnaturally yellowish). Neither saw him lurking nearby, or noticed him grabbing the kid's overcoat before hastily retreating.

Then he retreated further—departing Mission Park along the curvy paths that had brought him there, his steps bringing him closer to desert scrub and the railroad tracks.

Behind him now were the public toilet and the palm trees.

Somewhere up ahead, resting at the banks of an arroyo, was a rusty, abandoned four-door Maverick—no windshield, no engine, springs and fluff for cushions—where he would sleep until evening: his dreaming ineffable and black, yet lingering indescribably upon his waking, making him uneasy.

He'd go into the night wondering: Had Julie appeared? Was it something about Polo? My children?

Or did he dream of that billboard looming by the decrepit strip mall? How white and blank it was when he first visited the oriental market—only to be transformed a week later, filled with Rosas' stern gaze against a red background, the detective's index finger pointing, his message in bold letters above his head: BE A CRIME BUSTER, LET'S TAKE OUR CITY BACK!

Doesn't matter, he convinced himself while trudging down the arroyo. "Doesn't matter," he whispered, his shoes sinking in sand which shimmered from moonlight. He inhaled the dry night air, his skin soothed by a flat wind.

Soon the breezy nights and warm days passed as if each hour had somehow doubled in duration, yet he kept a moderate pace when traveling through the city—meandering past the Amtrak station where his Mazda had been parked, weaving leisurely amidst the downtown buildings, napping more than once within an alley just a block from Rosas' office. In that same alley he discovered a bag of stale bagels near a dumpster, a veritable feast which sustained him during his slow journey west.

He pressed onward, his spindly body cloaked with Barton's overcoat (a deterrent from the punishing sun, a safeguard from the increasingly cooler evenings). But his wandering didn't lack direction, rather he was forging a direct course and proceeding toward Papago Park—that sprawling oasis geographically opposed to Mission Park; it was a larger, more recent creation, offering four public toilets instead of one (an ideal place for cruising, he conceived, and a place where Polo might go).

So he moved assuredly—all the while resting during daylight, resuming his trek at night—and never once was he stopped by the police or harassed by anyone. Hardly realizing how adept he'd become, he slept easily against asphalt, on flattened cardboard boxes behind warehouses, inside concrete bunkers beneath highway overpasses.

Then at some point—after walking down sidewalks where no one met his eyes, after pausing in bustling crowds where faces floated by without a glance—he grasped the specter-like perception of those commonly seen as transients: to be a vagrant was to exist literally on the periphery of all sight; if the behavior wasn't erratic or the movements non-threatening, no acknowledgment was readily given. He was, perhaps, invisible and like a ghost too, and such a notion brought a little comfort—though not enough to sedate his longing for Julie and the children, or his desire to stand before his students or to build model airplanes; only enough to make him feel fairly anonymous and unimpeded as he went.

And that, he told himself, was truly worth something.

AT PAPAGO Park, when sleeping throughout the day, he rested in plain sight upon a bench, his head covered by Barton's overcoat. Yards away, in nearly every direction, stretched the bodies of others—sprawled beneath palm trees, zipped up inside sleeping bags—all scattered about the ample, obliging grounds (none slumbering too close to another, each claiming their own share of grass and shade). As expansive as Papago Park was, he quickly realized there was enough acreage for everyone: families, couples, joggers, and roller bladers could enjoy the front half of the park without ever noticing a weathered face; the transients could lurk much further back amongst the trails, along the desert fringes (disappearing if need be behind mesquite tree clusters, or the massive prickly pear groupings), where the unbroken turf gave way to sloping, rugged terrain.

Yet if Papago Park seemed an ideal haven for the homeless (much more so than the smaller Mission Park), it apparently wasn't a favored cruising spot. Perhaps, he thought, because of its remote location—or perhaps, in its newness, the park lacked the reputation of those well established gathering places. Perhaps, with Mission Park and the video arcade being easily accessible, no one had bothered to make the drive west, to arrive at what was obviously a safer environment for men to meet.

Still, in his month or so of staking out the various toilets around the park, he did observe a smattering of activity, none of it terribly explicit—though a suitable amount to encourage his notion that Polo might possibly be found there: an elderly gentleman repeatedly wandering in and out of a toilet one evening; the clearly effeminate teenager standing beside a drinking fountain for over an hour, glancing at a toilet entrance and never once bending to drink; the occasionally glimpsed solitary men strolling toward the toilets, pausing at picnic tables, reclining on nearby benches as if expecting someone.

But no Polo.

Then with the thickening of his beard, the spreading of his hair, so too grew a consuming resentment for his former companion, an increased loathing when he imagined Polo having dinner with a wife, playing with children, looking exactly like he always had (clean-cut, fit beneath his nice shirts, saturating the air with his cologne), remaining unchanged while he transformed into something wild, something pungent and far removed from that passport picture shown in the newspaper.

Goddammit, if I could just talk to you, he thought. If you could see me and see what has happened to me—if we could sit together like friends—if we could talk—

How he craved a mutual exchange, longed for the sound of someone's voice rather than the distant shouts of kids, the enthusiastic yells of college students throwing Frisbees. Since leaving the Amtrak station, he wouldn't actually converse with another person, aside from the irascible Barton, until Tobias approached him late one afternoon (searching for his dog, spouting nonsense). But in the weeks before encountering Tobias, he often mumbled to himself, answering his questions, muttering vague reassurances underneath his breath; however, his own utterances did little to ease his need for real communication, for the articulation of unimportant information, for the pleasure and ease of small talk.

"The weather is getting cooler, isn't it?"

"Yes, very."

"You doing okay?"

"Not bad, yourself?"

"I'm good, thank you."

As the days passed and as his stakeouts, superseded by the necessity of finding food, became less routine, the urge for conversation plagued him. On the afternoon in which Tobias emerged, he held a pay phone at the Safeway where he now regularly pilfered tortillas and cheese, and, after depositing his last quarter and dialing his home number, promptly hung up the receiver.

"Idiot," he cursed lowly, admonishing his contorted reflection in the pay phone's smudged chrome. "Moron," he said, "you idiot." Then, as if punishing himself, he left the store without taking anything.

Or did he go because, while standing at the pay phone, a former student had entered the Safeway—pushing a shopping cart, flanked by his parents, yet paying no attention to the itinerant fellow removing his last quarter from the coin slot?

"Careless idiot," he continued cursing, crossing the parking lot. "You're pointless, everything's pointless—"

He mumbled between suburban tracts designated for new homes, through weed-covered fields, into winding arroyos: It was all useless—finding Polo was useless—he'd never see Julie and David and Monica again—he'd spend a lifetime living outdoors, or someone would recognize him or he'd get arrested or he'd do something stupid—like calling home—

"You idiot—you want Rosas to get you, don't you—don't you?"

With only a Milky Way bar and a pack of Twizzlers for dinner, he finally calmed down at Papago Park, eating silently on his bench as evening loomed.

Already fall was beginning its cycle—the mesquites turning golden, the late afternoon light creating sharp contrasts, the inevitable evening breeze enriched by a woodsy, slightly smoky scent—and he couldn't recall how many days and nights had elapsed since seeing Julie and the children, or how long it'd been since he'd slept in a bed. Then he began shivering within the overcoat, his skin forming goose pimples as if anticipating the cold that hadn't quite fully arrived.

"Say, buddy, you seen my dog anywhere?"

The voice came from nowhere, surprising him. Glancing sideways, he spotted Tobias strolling toward the bench, walking bowlegged.

"She's Tina. She's my bitch, you know—"

As Tobias continued talking, he sized him up—two baseball caps, barefoot, frayed jean cuffs rolled to scabby knees.

"What's she look like?" he asked, meeting Tobias' gray eyes, but first swallowing a mouthful of candy bar. "What breed?"

Tobias' expression narrowed into puzzlement: "Can't really say—she ran off in Phoenix a while back, maybe Tempe. Sort of a little happy dog, pretty eyes, real energetic. Boy, she ran fast, that little dog—that bitch."

You're insane, he thought. You're nuts.

However, Tobias was clearly benign, his nervous chatter betraying an affable nature, and John—perplexed yet somewhat amused by his demeanor, anxious for any sort of conversation—felt relieved when he sat down on the bench (the old guy's eyes roving as he spoke, darting from John to the candy bar to John).

"It's a fine evening, ain't that right? It'll get cold later—'cept it's fine at this moment, ain't that right?"

Soon the remainder of the Milky Way would get shared, the Twizzlers split—then Tobias would talk while chewing, the inset lines upon his craggy face becoming deeper with the sun's setting: John listening warmly to an endless, rarely coherent discourse—government conspiracies ("They're buildin' entire secret cities underground—they made that AIDS, you know—), cattle with zippers sewn along their sides ("Genetic engineerin'—they're doin' it in Brazil right now—), and the ineffable Gotam.

"You got the fear of Gotam?"

"I don't know, maybe."

"You got to have that fear. Christ, you don't fear Gotam you're askin' for a heap of trouble."

"I guess so."

"You know it, that's right."

As dusk settled, Tobias sighed wearily. The Twizzlers were gone, so was the candy bar. Sounding saddened, he said he had to go collect wood: "It'll turn cold tonight, I think. Has a way of doing that, you know."

"Good luck," John told him.

"You too, buddy," Tobias said, rising from the bench.

"Thanks, I will."

Except the old guy didn't readily move on—rather he scratched his chin, studying a flock of birds silhouetted in the sky before glancing toward John, saying, "Say, you know, I got me a nice place—not too bad, a sight better than that bench I keep seeing you on—got a nice fire there most nights, a bag you'd probably like resting in—and I've sure enjoyed you, buddy."

John looked at him, confused.

"You're welcome is what I'm tellin' you—you're welcome if you want—that's about it, I suppose—if you're interested is all—"

"You sure?" John asked. "You don't mind—?"

"Can't say I do on account that I don't—and you'll see, it ain't bad, you know—a lot nicer than that bench—all you got to do is follow—"

So, without deliberation, he followed, although second thoughts began ruminating once the palm trees were behind him.

Then the earth sloped downward into a wide arroyo, away from the park's boundary, and sand squished beneath his shoes, the grass appearing only as straggling clumps amongst the brownish loam.

Presently, when it seemed they were reaching a dead end, Tobias stopped and pointed up ahead: "Home—that's my place. You'll like it—"

In the evening light, he discerned very little, other than the arroyo severed by a towering hilly terrain of dirt and red stone and concrete (on top of which stretched asphalt, a highway that curved around the park).

"Not so bad," Tobias said, proceeding. "Could be worse—"

Suddenly, he saw the circular opening in the earth, the black portal beginning where the arroyo concluded.

"You'll like it, you'll see—the rent's cheap—"

By dark that tunnel would already feel hospitable and safe (there was fire, there was coffee, there was agreeable company). In time an implicit arrangement would get reached: twice a week John stole food for himself and Tobias, his reimbursement being the loan of a sleeping bag, his share of water from Tobias' gallon jug, and the old guy's pleasant rambling which, if not always rational, sporadically rang true.

"Just germs, you know, keepin' folks from treatin' us kinder—scared of germs, I think, so they'll keep a distance from our types—if there aren't no germs or filth the world might overflow with compassion, ain't that right? 'Cept you and me know you don't got to look filthy to be filthy—and you can stay unwashed and stay a lot cleaner than a ton others who aren't, you know?"

"I suppose so."

"There you go, that's right—that's what I'm talkin' about—"

In a way, Tobias' companionship halved John's misery for a while; he could talk with someone, he could listen, and he could, at least until nightfall, forget his troubles for a time. Only when Tobias slept, snoring within his sleeping bag, did he find himself missing his family, or pondering

Polo's whereabouts, or damning Rosas. Sitting awake by the fire, he'd stir the cinders, sometimes picturing the detective on his trail—roaming across Papago Park, coming closer and closer.

My Javert, he has thought, while also envisioning the tunnel as a Paris sewer (year after year he had taught *Les Miserables*, never foreseeing that his life would someday resemble Hugo's drama). And like Jean Valjean, he too was just a minor criminal, hardly worthy of pursuit by such an incorruptible policeman. All the same, there was something heroic, something oddly enlivening about being so misunderstood—and there at the fire he'd quietly repeat what he had often spoken aloud to his students, the words upon Valjean's neglected and anonymous tombstone:

He sleeps. Although fate was very strange to him,
He lived. He died when he lost his angel;
It happened simply, as naturally as
The night falls when the day goes away.

Yet in the aftermath of what eventually transpired, he would never again feel an affinity for Jean Valjean, nor would he imagine savoring the kind of redemption Valjean had enjoyed during his final moments. No, he'd never have the chance to sacrifice his remaining happiness and have it returned a hundredfold—for he was ruined not wholly by circumstances but by his own feverish desperation, and, as he has now resigned himself to it, his true fate will surely be that of the lonely, the outcast, those who are destined to be forever deprived of the joy they once had, a joy unrealized until it disappeared. Therefore, in the end, he abandoned any kinship whatsoever with Hugo's hero, ultimately finding little common ground other than that he and Valjean were human to a fault.

Except I am more so, he concluded. There are no happy endings for me—what could be more human than that?

But if it wasn't entirely destiny which had brought about his complete undoing, he at least believed coincidence played a role. Possibly it was a strange form of serendipity. Or maybe neither pure coincidence or serendipity were involved; rather it was something else born of the two, something less definable and specific.

He recalled his cousin's holiday in Aspen, how she rode the ski lift by herself and, gazing at the run below, watched as someone skied recklessly into a pine tree—an accidental death she alone witnessed, one which meant interviews with the police, several tearful telephone calls, and an abrupt finish to her trip.

When returning home, she was e-mailed by the victim's Texan parents, both mother and father wanting information regarding their daughter's last seconds. In time, the following would get pieced together: a young secretary from Dallas had taken an Aspen vacation and was killed skiing into a tree; the only person to see her death was her boss' stepdaughter, a graphic arts designer who lived in San Diego and who, like the secretary, was also on vacation (an inexplicable connection which left his cousin shaken for months).

Then, there was his college roommate, a fellow English student who, falling under the spell of mystical literature, endeavored to read the collected works of Kahlil Gibran. The day after completing his goal he attended a professor's gallery opening, where, while mingling with strangers, he struck up a conversation with a Mr. Gibran, an elderly art collector visiting friends in Arizona.

"I don't suppose you're related to the Lebanese writer?" his roommate asked when he learned the art collector's name.

"Why of course," came the emphatic answer. "He was my uncle."

Such curious encounters had occurred throughout his life, usually to others he knew. But they aren't meaningless, he told himself. Nor were they simply mere coincidence or just happenstance—instead, for him, they hinted at some grand meaning, an indication that all human beings are guided here and there by an irresistible power, like chess pieces moved across a vast board toward carefully plotted, though rarely certain, fates.

How else to explain his student from Chile who, by chance, bumped into her long-lost childhood friend when visiting Disneyland; or Julie exploring antique stores in vain for a replica Mammy cookie jar, finding one a week later (albeit badly cracked and needing repair), inside a cardboard box set beside their alley trash bin; or the colleague who lost his wedding ring while jogging (his subsequent hunt for it involving flashlights, the retracing of each place his sneakers fell), discovering it weeks afterwards on the finger of a clueless teaching assistant: "Can you believe what I found at the park?"

Or, while perhaps less remarkable, John strolling along a Safeway aisle, keeping his head lowered as shoppers walked by, and suddenly inhaling the passing fragrance of cologne (the very same smell which had drawn him repeatedly into the back stall, the smell he now associated with hope). Then, as if materializing when the search had seemingly become futile, there went Polo—moving leisurely away, pushing a shopping cart down the aisle—his tan Dockers unmistakable beneath the vivid fluorescence.

But Polo, appearing so unassuming and ordinary, wasn't unaccompanied: a small girl with strawberry blond hair, no more than five, sat within the cart and amongst groceries; an attractive woman—tall, reddish hair, slender and tanned—preceded the cart like a scout, casually surveying the shelves ahead.

For a while he stood inert, stupefied by the emergence of Polo, unsure of what to do next—because, he realized, the context was completely wrong; in his mind, they were supposed to meet again at Mission Park or at Papago Park, somewhere unlit and discreet, but not inside a bright grocery store, never around that many people. Still, he remained calm—his heart didn't race, his hands didn't shake.

Was it even Polo? he wondered. Could he be positive, especially since he had glimpsed him previously in darkness, amid shadows and the night?

Polo paused, turning slightly, reaching for a box of granola bars, his wedding band made visible, his lips pursing as he studied the box: "I love it up here," he had told John the night they drove to the overlook. "I love being here with you," he'd said, bringing those lips closer.

Yes, John thought, it's you.

Yes, without question it was him: so he began following, maintaining a careful distance (confident that, should Polo glance back, nothing familiar could be seen behind his heavy overcoat and thick beard, his vagrant face). Yet in hindsight, he has wished he'd run for the pay phone outside and dialed 911 as planned, except that, fearing Polo might disappear again, he didn't dare risk leaving him. Moreover, he was entranced by their domesticity—the way Polo and the woman added groceries to the cart (coffee filters, pasta shells, Pringles), the small girl pointing indiscriminately at the shelves, saying aloud, "Please buy that—buy that, okay?"

Up and down the aisles he trailed them, his envy growing rancorous with every item placed within the cart, thinking to himself: How can you sleep, knowing what they've done to me? How can you live comfortably keeping your secrets, at the same time taking for granted these things I no longer have—the shopping, the errands, the mundane family rituals?

But, he was convinced, Polo wouldn't sleep easily after that evening. Come morning, Rosas would enter his life as well—all he had to do was follow them from the store, see which car they climbed into, memorize the license number, then leave a message on the detective's voice mail ("Now you can finally let me be, now you can stop persecuting me!").

He would have done exactly that had Polo not left the cart, walking briskly by himself toward the rear of the Safeway, hands deep in his pockets. Even so, he stayed behind him like a magnet, moving across the store—past the fresh produce section, past the meat department—through swinging black doors which lead into a long narrow corridor: Polo proceeded without ever turning around, without ever knowing his steps were being dogged—never breaking his stride even when pushing open the door of the men's restroom and wandering inside.

Hesitating in the corridor, John drew a breath—inhaling his own solitude, exhaling his resolve—aware that no one else roamed nearby (the others were somewhere beyond the swinging black doors, customers and employees busily taking care of what must be done). Then he entered the restroom, going where Polo had gone, shuffling over white tiles, pausing beside the row of sinks—where, for a second, he was relieved to find no one else present. Gazing about, he found himself counting the toilet stalls (three), the sinks (four), the mirrors (four), the liquid soap dispensers (two), the urinals (five). However, he wouldn't really contemplate the differences between the Safeway restroom and the Mission Park toilet until afterwards: how well lit it was here, how modern and accommodating—the floor mopped, the sinks scrubbed and like new.

He stooped, peeking underneath the stall partitions, and spotted Polo's loafers in the back toilet, his Dockers bunched at his ankles (of course, he thought, of course—); three vacant stalls, three options, yet habit had brought him to the most secluded toilet. So he would wait for Polo's exit, at long last greeting him there in that restroom: as good a place as any to talk, he reasoned. Almost as discreet as Mission Park.

Approaching the back stall, he listened while Polo fumbled with tissue paper, wiping clean those nerve endings his fingertips had once caressed. Shortly thereafter, Polo stood, pulling up his pants, fastening his belt—then the toilet flushed. And when the stall door swung open, John's despairing form blocked passage, his unexpected presence startling Polo.

You'll help me, were the whispered words immediately spoken: You must help me.

"Excuse me," Polo said, taken aback. "Excuse me," he said again, attempting to squeeze by.

John didn't appear to hear him, nor would he let Polo leave. Sweat shimmered on his forehead, glistened in his beard. It was Polo who had to wait now, he said, because he had waited long enough. It was Polo who he had been trying to find: "Now you'll help me."

Except Polo's expression showed no sign of sympathy or recognition, only apprehension and fear—a flinching mistrust for the stranger before him, the disheveled man keeping him trapped within the stall.

"I'm sorry—will you please let me go—?"

He placed a palm flat on Polo's chest. "It's me," he whispered. "You know me."

"Look, I don't know you, all right? Move—"

"Can't you see, it's me," he interrupted, nudging Polo further into the stall. "From Mission Park." He moved inside. "Every Thursday and Saturday." He shut the stall door, locking it, and, with their chests touching, whispered, "It's me."

Just then he believed Polo's lips parted with recognition, but almost as quickly the recognition became masked by refusal: "I'm sorry—"

Even while he gazed at him hopefully, even as he implored him.

"I'm sorry—you have me confused—"

Even knowing the truth, even as he pled his case ("Without you I've got nothing, I can't clear my name, I'm stuck—but if you'll go with me to the detective, tell him— it won't take much time and it'll save me—and your family won't ever hear a word, I promise.").

"I'm sorry, I don't know what you're talking about— really, I can't help you!"

So he begged, saying please please please please like a child verging on a tantrum.

"Listen, I can't help you, don't you understand?"

"Please, I've got no one, I've got nowhere to go—I've tried finding you for the longest time—help me."

Polo nodded, his eyes squinting as if considerations were getting weighed. Then a soothing hand rested upon John's shoulder: "All right, I can at least do something for you, okay?"

"Thank you," John said, and, for a moment, he sensed those rainy afternoons at the Mission Park toilet with Polo, those minutes in the back stall which now seemed so dreamlike and ideal.

"I can help a little."

The hand drifted from John's shoulder, disappearing behind Polo, reappearing with a wallet. Then he watched in disbelief as two dollar bills materialized, pinched between Polo's fingers.

"This is all I can do for you."

Polo took his hand, pressing the bills into it.

"This will help some—now do you mind?"

"I don't need your money."

"Listen, I'm being patient but you're wasting my time, please move or I'll make you move."

As Polo returned the wallet into its pocket, John let the dollars fall to the floor: "Don't deny me—don't you dare— I need you—-"

Polo had had enough; he bore into John, grabbing for the stall lock, only to be repelled by a forceful shove backwards.

"Don't deny me—"

"Let me out," Polo said, exasperated. "You let me out or I'll turn you in, I'll call the police and say you assaulted me, got it?"

John shook his head, saying nothing.

Once more Polo went for the lock in vain, throwing himself against John, yelling, "Help! Help—!"

"Shut up," he hissed, panicking. "Shut up!"

"Someone—please—!"

How he hated Polo just then, how he despised the sight of him—the coward, no different than Rosas, no different than Julie, as useless and unforgiving and cruel as the rest.

"Someone—"

"Shut—up—!"

Later, he would revise his own memory, reconfiguring what he scarcely believed was true: as it had really happened, he was sure that he'd been incapable of grasping Polo's neck so tightly when they began struggling.

"Don't deny me, you won't deny me—".

He hadn't clutched and clutched and clutched with such hatred, with such contempt and blame.

"Fuck you, fuck you—"

Nor did Polo, after a brief fight, abruptly stop resisting, as if his body had suddenly accepted John's venom.

"Fuckers, all of you—you've ruined me—"

The hands didn't finally uncoil, sliding from that neck reddened by unimaginable pressure—the fingers didn't seize the discarded bills, crumpling them and stuffing them past Polo's discolored lips, far into his faintly gurgling throat.

"Shut up—just shut up—"

There weren't those vacuous staring eyes, the pliable body slumped awkwardly upon the toilet seat.

"Goddamn you—"

None of it had occurred.

Still, regardless of how he tried, he couldn't forget his feverish digging into Polo's pocket, his fingers finding the wallet and yanking it out.

Who are you? he wondered.

With trembling hands, he gripped credit cards and family photos (Polo posing beside the woman, Polo standing behind the girl, Polo as a soccer coach surrounded by prepubescent boys); he opened folded bits of paper inscribed with hastily written phone numbers and e-mail account passwords; he sorted through various video membership cards, a Firestone Buy 3 Oil Changes Get 1 Free punch coupon—until, at last, Polo's driver's license came to light (not Polo, no, never Polo—Michael A. Fitzpatrick instead, birthdate: 09/16/63).

Michael A. Fitzpatrick—the name etching itself across his brain, engraved on his memory, along with the home address (1492 South Frontera St., a street he had traveled along on his way to and from the high school). Both name and address obliterating any other thoughts, each repeated lowly again and again as he fled the stall, as he exited the restroom and ran from the store—as he went senselessly into the evening, thinking nothing yet of the body he had left or coming face to face with a deli clerk when racing down the corridor (the afterimage of the bewildered clerk's eyes lingering momentarily, those prominent brown pupils fixing on him) or the security cameras which had recorded his quick departure, saying only to himself, "Michael A. Fitzpatrick, fourteen ninety-two Frontera Street—Michael A. Fitzpatrick—"

HE RUSHED toward the desert, running blindly through a desolate construction site, along dirt avenues yet to be paved, past the hollow frames of suburban homes in various states of creation, the beams and planks crisscrossing in the dusky sky. Behind him sirens started blaring, one followed by another and another and another. Then it seemed as if the sirens were drawing closer and pursuing him.

As he ran headlong with labored breath, he gripped Fitzpatrick's driver's license, unaware of the thick plastic laminate cutting into his hand. His legs already burned but hadn't grown weak, and, while not conscious of the thin cuts forming across his palm, he knew the weeks of long walking were now serving him well.

At the fringes of the construction site, he burst into an orange grove, squashing the fallen fruit underfoot, stumbling repeatedly among the trees. Each staggered row was like the last—the trees equal in height, spaced exactly apart—and this disoriented him. The countless, almost identical branches and leaves meshed before him, obscuring everything except the stars above; the pointed offshoots stretched out in all directions, often grazing his neck and head. As if navigating a maze, he scrambled from row to row in the darkness, attempting to keep his bearings even when struck or scratched by the fruit-laden branches. How maddening it was knowing that the desert was so very near, yet so difficult to reach.

However, he eventually found his way from the orange grove, and, lurching forward, his field of vision became more expansive: before him was a barbed-wire fence, beyond it lay the desert and the black-blue sky. While carefully grasping the twisted wire, he realized he no longer held the driver's license, envisioning it now lost somewhere in the rows when he'd tripped. The slack top wire lifted easily, and, pressing the bottom wire down with a shoe, he passed through to the other side of the fence—where, for a moment, he paused to catch his breath, and saw the barren scrub brush scattered ahead as far as he could see, appearing like tufts of straw beneath the stark moonlight.

Suddenly he felt the wind—a light breeze weaving across the desert, patting his overcoat as he quickened his pace and began running again. In time the city lights glowed in the distance, the sirens long since quieted—but he kept moving away, brushing against prickly pears, maneuvering around saguaros, pounding over rocks, tripping while he went.

Finally unable to go any further, he came to a place where a hilly clearing was encompassed by brittle wild grass. A cluster of barren mesquite trees, sheltering the wild grass, prevented easy access to the hill and stood as a craggy barrier. The towering, curious shapes of saguaros occupied the edge of the clearing, standing before the wild grass and mesquites as if keeping them at bay.

Here silence prevailed—save for the wind and the wild grass rustling—and he sat in the clearing exhausted, his skull throbbing with blood, his lungs spent, his arms and legs shaking with adrenaline. Then he welcomed the frigid air which had increased since nightfall, cooling the sweat on his face, making his breath float past his lips like steam rising from asphalt. Soon the cold crept inside the overcoat, slowing his mind and numbing his skin. But the chill hadn't quite hindered his guard, his watchfulness: behind the mesquites, behind the swaying wild grass, behind the tall saguaros with their sharp needles and wide trunks, he knew that obscured figures waited and lurked unseen, though the night was luminous, the moon shining into the branches and stems, and the desert reflecting its whiteness; he sensed their presence, but was too fatigued to avoid them.

At last unable to stay upright, he slumped backwards toward the ground—glimpsing the heavens as he fell, a blurring of starlight—and struck the base of his skull against a rock. A deadening sensation enveloped him, shooting to the extremities of his body.

So I have killed myself, he thought while moaning aloud. I've done it by chance and it ends for me here.

Half-aware now in the clearing, he writhed upon the ground—violently at first, then less so—until he could move no more. Inhaling the air, the cold stinging his nostrils, he wondered why he subsisted.

Or perhaps, he wondered, he had already died. Perhaps he had been dead for weeks, meandering as one who imagined himself alive. Perhaps he, like everyone else, had been mistaken: consciousness didn't cease with death, and death didn't bring life to an end.

So the dead might always persist, walking without voice, forever unnoticed, somehow alive and making choices. Dead or living, the wind would still touch the skin and raise goose pimples—the sun would burn the face, the night would bring sleep.

Alive or dead, he thought, there is no difference—the suffering remains.

"I'm dead now too," he whispered, his body becoming lax. "I'm just like all of you—"

Emerging through the mesquite trees they came— gliding toward him, crushing the wild grass with their shoes, laughing as they approached. Shutting his eyes, he wasn't frightened. Instead, he delighted in their laughter when drifting off, and felt soothed by their company, those people beside whose corpses he had stood: his father and Banister and Fitzpatrick—the laughing dead.

At once sleep overtook him, subduing him completely, sending him elsewhere for a time.

Shortly thereafter, he would stir in a bed shared with his wife and children, and he would find himself staring at their sleeping faces in the moonlight. Before they woke, he'd tell them goodbye, saying so to each—bye Julie, bye David, bye Monica.

He'd walk naked toward snow-capped mountains, ambling over dry sand. Nearby was an adobe village set within a riparian area, where black dogs walked like men and barked furiously at him, and two Mexican women stitched yarn patterns on the backs of shirtless children. The sun would then vanish in a cloud of crimson dust, the wind and sand consuming all.

He'd sit meditatively somewhere on that snow-capped mountain beneath a pine tree, seeing himself there and noticing how his skin had turned as brown and as coarse as leather, his body emaciated. He'd follow himself down the mountainside, and realize it wasn't himself he was following but someone else.

He'd squint at a window illuminated by a brilliant golden light, and he'd hear someone faintly calling his name outside.

Having lost his hearing and eyesight, he'd panic in his mother's kitchen and, in his malady, vomit a shimmering red foam on the black-and-white linoleum.

A thorn would stick painfully into his chin, and he'd run along a path in a field of tall green grass, listening to hymns sung through what sounded like a megaphone. Then his own body would become that of a boy's body, and he'd tell himself that he needed to take a deep breath, he needed to calm himself by tugging a fingernail with his teeth, pulling at it until it came off and the skin underneath began unraveling like thread in a ball of twine. There on the path he'd no longer be the boy and he'd promptly leave him, glancing back every so often and observing how much of the ragged skin was piling up around the boy's feet, vaguely amused at the exposed bone and tendons of the boy's flailing mess of an arm.

He'd climb from a cot and drink a glass of water.

He'd reach for a door knob, but somehow be incapable of actually touching it.

"Here," Polo would say, bending to tie his sneakers. "I'll do it." Polo's hair was red, then white. Polo stood, facing him, and his complexion had turned dark brown. "See, it's me," Polo told him, covering his face with his hands. "It's always been me—can't you tell?"

Later, Tobias would cradle his head, feeding him watery rice with a plastic spoon, wiping his lips with a napkin. Except Tobias looked like his father, and he felt safe being held by him. The rice would clear his mind, Tobias told him. The rice would help him regain his strength. "All human beings must eat," said Tobias.

Awaking in the bright morning, he sat up amongst the desert scrub.

Glancing about uncertainly, he became aware of the haphazard saguaros encircling him here and there, as if they had been keeping guard during his sleep, their various long shadows slanting westward, shading him. He pulled his legs against his chest, absently removing prickly pear needles from his trouser cuffs. After a time he stood, rubbing the tender gash on his head in the sharp light.

All around him the creosote bushes and cacti and deadwood blazed with flaxen hues, each underscored by dark patches on the earth.

Cheeping birds paced mesquite branches, or perched high atop saguaros, or bobbed through the sky, while jackrabbits and tiny ground squirrels roamed about nearby like soldiers cautiously traversing a minefield, pausing to sniff at the dirt before proceeding.

Something terrible has happened again, he suddenly remembered.

Something unforeseen and damaging—but not of his doing, no.

He gazed across the desert, realizing then how far he had come (six miles perhaps, possibly further), arriving here without the ease of a trail and by having forged his own aimless path amid prickly pears, fuzzy cholla, brush weeds, and thousands of jagged red rocks.

Behind him now sloped mountainous terrain, cleaving the flatlands, dotted with saguaros.

Below him in the valley, just visible on the pale blue horizon, were the hazy shapes of the city skyline; closer still, he spotted the distant palm trees of Papago Park, then the duck pond glimmering dully—its water inanimate and murky, indistinct even when touched by such glorious sunlight.

Michael A. Fitzpatrick, he thought. That poor stranger, those lifeless eyes.

He had tried frantically to revive him, to bring him back (his hands pressing flesh while uttering please please please please)—but, as had been the case with Banister, Michael A. Fitzpatrick was already dead before John found him in the back stall.

He continued surveying the desert, sensing the inevitable wind which would sweep in from the west or down from the north, muting everything save its own resonance, abruptly shaking the stems and branches, stirring the hard dirt that lay within the dark patches and scattering it yonder and rendering it thoroughly into dust.

Yet how could it happen again? he wondered.

How could he stumble upon another body, another victim of that faceless monster who had killed Banister—and why was this person persecuting him so, always ensnaring him? Is it you, Rosas? Are you the one? Are my sins that abhorrent that I should pay like this?

He began walking, his legs aching as he went, telling himself that Polo would surely be found. Polo alone knew the truth, and Polo, of all people, would explain to everyone that he hadn't killed Banister and therefore he hadn't killed Michael A. Fitzpatrick (just bad luck finding both bodies, a coincidence, maybe a set-up). He is gentle by nature, Polo would reveal. He is considerate, couldn't hurt a fly. He is my friend and I value him.

He imagined Polo with his black hair (or was it brown?), his green eyes (or were they blue?), his dim face obscured in the darkness of the Mission Park toilet—only superficially resembling Michael A. Fitzpatrick, only alike in their attire and choice of cologne.

Already the day was warming. The sun was dissipating the night's chill and warming his brow and forming mirages on the desert plains. The cold that had disoriented him was gone and he felt clearheaded and, willing it to be, he glimpsed Polo several yards away, rushing in his direction. Then, promptly transforming before him, Polo became a large crow which sailed directly overhead.

He called for him, yelling for him to come back.

Standing motionless in that smoldering sunlight, he stared at the sky and saw Polo fade into the blue ether.

Soon Polo moved fleetingly within a grouping of mesquite trees, disappearing before being reached.

Soon Polo's steps fell behind him, crunching in tandem on pebbles—except when he swung around Polo had, as always, not been there.

After a while he sat on the ground, lowering his head and cupping his face in his hands. But he couldn't cry, regardless of how much he wanted to; he wouldn't let himself, he couldn't.

Or maybe it was the quaking of the earth which had stopped him, coupled with an intensifying roar that swelled in the sky like a fast-approaching wave. Raising his face from his hands, he watched astonished as two sleek F-16s soared toward him, flying low above the desert.

At that moment he felt incredibly at peace, as though somehow he was an intrinsic part of the wilderness surrounding him (tranquil, bending effortlessly, thriving under inhospitable conditions yet replete with existence): He was a small thing, he concluded. He was insignificant. In the universe, on this planet, here—he was simply a minuscule thing of little importance, and what he'd done or hadn't done was pointless—he was a small thing, a rogue bee, and no matter what would come of him, the world would continue to rotate a minor star in a minor galaxy in an infinite universe.

And afterwards, when the planes had vanished over the horizon, he arose and pressed onward, heading for the tunnel where he now sleeps near the fire and dreams nothing—where, come summer, he knows the monsoon rains will fall swiftly once again and, without any inclination, wash the tunnel clean of whatever has since proclaimed it as home.